# Kama Sutr
# Positions Guide

## *6 Books in 1*

*The #1 Guide on Kama Sutra with OVER 250+ Illustrated Sex Positions | Spicy Games, Hot Ideas & Dirty Talk. Beginners & Advanced Friendly.*

**Lana Fox**

# Table of contents

# TANTRIC SEX TECHNIQUES

Tantric sex aims at the full sharing of emotions, sensations, both physical and mental. It unhinges the voracity typical of modern sexuality, understood as a pure vehicle of carnal pleasure, aimed at achieving a pleasant orgasm. Calmness, slowness and sharing are the basis, instead, of this doctrine that aims, as an objective, the improvement of sexuality, always, as clarified, passing from awareness and sharing of feelings and emotions.

The tantra practices focus, in fact, on the visual attention of the lovers, on tactile sensations, passing through the symbiosis of breath. Movement and rhythm, especially in the part of the pelvis, are the key words of tantric sex, these are what put in circulation a lot of energy, more than what we think we hide inside us, allowing us to unlock them, renewing the pleasure of the senses and the inner one. Tantric sex aims to allow those who practice it to better know both their body and that of their partner, encouraging the harmony of the couple.

## The Tantric Massage: What Is It & How To Do It

Tantric massage is an ancient Indian practice that promotes the understanding of oneself and others by light and circular touches, leading to a feeling of well-being that is both union and liberation: let's look at all the benefits.

Through tantric massage and stimulation of certain energy points of the figure. It provides a tremendous deal of sensory pleasure as well as an improvement in self-perception and self-esteem to the individual who receives it. That is good to increase the knowledge and harmony of the couple. Tantric massage is based on ancient Indian teachings, which in turn date back to texts of pre-vedic cultures, the origin of which is still quite mysterious and controversial. The ancient population of the Harappa, for example, put significant attention to tantra's energy, particularly the female form and its element, water; in the middle of their homes, there was a large swimming pool and a room with a large bed on which to conduct tantric massage.

## How To Do The Tantric Massage

The tantric massage is structured in three phases.

> In the first phase we focus on meditation and meditation, creating in a suitable and intimate place, such as the bedroom, a cozy environment, with soft lighting, incense, practicing breathing exercises and reciting mantras.

> The second phase is focused on slow, circular and light massages on face and body, from legs to arms, passing through the pelvic area, back, neck and head, with gentle touches along the vital energy channels, chakras and nadi. A warm and delicate vector oil, such as coconut oil, is used.

> The last phase is relaxation: sipping a warm herbal tea you share the experience with those who have practiced it, verbalizing what you have experienced. Advantages of tantric massage.

## All The Benefits Of Tantric Massage

Everyone can enjoy advantages and benefits, including a new experience of sexuality, not limited in space and time, but perceived as omnipresent energy to be channeled into every cell of the body. In this way, anxiety, stress concerns are dissolved, along with other tensions.

Far from being a sexual practice, tantric massage acts on the genitals by dissolving blockages and going to relax the first chakra, using Tantra lingam techniques for men and Tantra yoni for women. There is also the technique of Tantra Kundalini massage. Tantric massage, a practice aiming at rediscovering the sanctity of the body as an element and physical envelope of the soul, combines personal growth and sensory experiences targeted at well-being.

# Tantra Kundalini Massage

This is one of the most curious, fascinating and sensual forms of tantra massage: we are talking about the Kundalini technique, which ideally represents a snake, which in turn symbolizes the primordial energies that reside in each of us, to be precise at the first chakra. The snake is the metaphor of transformation, in reference to its peculiarity of losing and rebuilding the skin regularly, and the transformation is associated with well-being in physical and spiritual terms as well as enlightenment (remember that the tantra philosophy aims at the elevation of the individual).

The Kundalini tantric massage, in particular, awakens the primordial energy of the first chakra - located in the perineal area - the starting point for a tantra massage that also involves the genital areas, without excluding any part of the body, until reaching the seventh chakra, the top of the neck.

During the Kundalini tantra massage the chakras should be progressively purified, so that the Kundalini - i.e. primordial energy - can get the upper hand by breaking down obstacles such as attachment to physical and material pleasure (this is linked to sexual intercourse seen as an act of donation not necessarily aimed at orgasm), as well as to our ego. At the moment of Kundalini's awakening, in the recipient of this specific tantra massage, thanks to the harmonious and enveloping movements with which it is massaged, the entire body will experience a feeling of complete well-being and total pleasure.

The effectiveness of the massage can be achieved thanks to very prolonged manipulations (even two hours) performed by an experienced operator: do not try this massage without mastering the technique perfectly. The purpose of the massage is to promote relaxation of the muscles adjacent to the spine, to prepare the central channel (sushumua) to welcome the upward flow of kundalini energy. Once the back, shoulders and neck are open, the lower back, including legs, feet and buttocks, must be massaged vigorously to release tension in the lower extremities to facilitate kundalini upward flow.

With the back of the body relaxed, the lower pelvic area is prepared to be relaxed and opened through a circular deep massage into the sacral and pelvic area. In this way the main natii or astral canal is purified so that the kundalini currents can flow and join the Vishnu. The direction is always from bottom to top. For this reason, the work on the body starts at the bottom. The chakra centers are opened and balanced in order, from the bottom, then from the muladhara chakra, to the other, through the other chakra centers to the sahasrara. This opening serves to prepare the body for further releases and movements of kundalini energy.

When the lower pelvic cavity begins to open thanks to deep massage, the upper chakra siri must be prepared with gentle touches along the thorn in the direction of the neck. The highest chakra, ajna, and the Sahasrara area at the top of the head, are prepared for the opening through an energetic balance obtained without contact with the body. The opening of the subsequent chakras will create a passage that will allow the kundalini to radiate upwards. This first part of the massage, in which the recipient is lying face down, is preparatory to the second part, in which he will be lying on his back.

Once the chakra centers are activated, the kundalini energy contained in the muldhara chakra, placed at the base of the column, is gently released. The kundalini energy is often called "snake energy" because it lies inert, coiled at the base of the vertebral axis; it is static and sealed at the root of the spine, just beyond the tip of the sacrum. Releasing this energy creates two forces, one centripetal (Shakti) and the other centrifugal (Shiva). Shakti is directed upward to the highest chakras, to complete a union with Shiva. whose original source, according to Tantra, is the sun. It is thanks to the union of these two forces that harmony and balance are achieved, according to ancient Tantric beliefs.

Often the first experience of releasing kundalini energy is disappointing: the energy hardly rises above the first or second chakra. However, after a number of sessions that varies from subject to subject, the release of "awakened" kundalini energy takes place: those who have experienced it describe it as an unforgettable experience, in which one perceives a sort of liquid fire flowing up the sushumna, through the head and the top of the body.

## MULTIPLE ORGASM
The orgasm isn't the cherry on top for many people when it comes to lovemaking. It's the entire sundae. They treat foreplay and intercourse as if there were playing poker, and if they play their cards right, they win the pot and cash those chips in for a mind-blowing, body quivering orgasm.

What if they don't climax? Well, then they treat the whole experience as though they won the pot only to discover the chips can't be cashed in. They're stuck with two handfuls of cheap plastic. Everyone can agree that orgasms feel amazing. It's a sure sign that all the elements in lovemaking came together correctly to give that partner a moment of ecstasy.

As great as they are, it's a huge mistake to make that the goal of lovemaking, especially when practicing the Kama Sutra. When practicing the techniques, the experience shouldn't judge whether or not one or both partners experienced orgasms. They shouldn't even be basing it on how close they came to climaxing. Orgasms can be very elusive, especially for women. Sometimes thinking about it makes it difficult actually to have it. Sometimes, it doesn't happen because it just didn't happen.

### Male Orgasm Basics
The male orgasm is something that most people have witnessed or seen if they have ever watched porn or heard about it in the media. The male orgasm is made to be extremely simple and easy to achieve, but in this part, we will examine it in more detail and break it down into more specific pieces.

To start, are you aware that there are different types of male orgasms? You are probably aware of this if you are a male, but you may not be a female. The term male orgasm includes any and every type of orgasm that involves the male's genitals.

## Orgasm and Ejaculation

Ejaculation and orgasm for males are two different events, even though they most often happen simultaneously. This fact makes them often misunderstood, as many think that ejaculation is a sign of orgasm. If orgasm occurs and ejaculation co-occurs, this is called an ejaculatory orgasm.

There is another type of orgasm that happens when ejaculation does not. As you likely guessed, this type is called a non-ejaculatory orgasm. That is sometimes called dry orgasm, which is also very typical. A man can achieve orgasm without ejaculation, which counts as an orgasm.

## How to Stimulate the Prostate to Achieve Orgasm

Once you have found the prostate, you can massage this area and let the sensations build gently. Keep going like this and determine what type of movements or pressure feels best. As you continue to stimulate it, let the pleasure make to the point of orgasm. When you are comfortable with this spot, try having your partner encourage it for you. Having someone else's hands touch it for you will feel different than your own, and with your free hand, you can turn yourself and your partner on in other ways.

The prostate is sometimes referred to as the male G-Spot. It has many similar properties to the female G-Spot, such as how you can find it and how it needs t to be stimulated to reach orgasm.

## Female Orgasm Basics

To make a woman orgasm, you will need to know and understand the female body, including all places where, when stimulated, a woman will feel pleasure and maybe even orgasm. Both sexes can learn more about the female body, whether you are a female or a male with a female partner.

## How to Stimulate the Clitoris to Achieve Orgasm

Once you have found the clitoris, you will stimulate it to achieve orgasm. Begin by gently placing two fingers on it and putting a bit of pressure. Rub it by moving your fingers in small circles-making sure to be gentle. Continue to do this, and she should begin to get more aroused the more you do this. By rubbing the clitoris, you will be able to stimulate the entire clitoris, even the part that you cannot see, which will cause the woman to start to become wet in her vaginal area for her body to prepare for sex.

## How to Stimulate the G-Spot to Achieve Orgasm

To give a woman pleasure by stimulating her G-Spot, you will need to press on it repeatedly until she reaches orgasm. That can be done using your fingers, a penis, or sex toys of various sorts. The G-Spot needs to receive continued and consistent stimulation for the pleasure to build enough for her to reach orgasm.

Since a woman can have two different types of orgasms, one from stimulating the clitoris and a different one from penetration or hitting the G-spot, this could be why a woman can reach orgasm during oral sex, or by having her clitoris stimulated but has trouble getting the same level of pleasure during penetrative sex. In many positions, the G-spot is not produced by the man's penis, resulting in the woman having some fun but not enough to reach orgasm. For a great experience as a couple, knowing what makes the woman feel great is paramount.


## Sex Toys: A Guide To Choosing The Right One

Sex toys are many and different in materials, sizes, and even prices: finding the right sex toy for you and your fantasies may not be easy, here are the useful advice.

### Sex toy: where to buy it

In addition to the classic men's sex shops - where, however, many couples are also supplied and where you can also find objects with a more refined design - sex toys can also be found:

- in pharmacies, where the offer is quite limited...
- in the lingerie and underwear department of some department stores...
- in sex shops and online boutiques
- in erotic boutiques, where discretion and advice between women are guaranteed.

Choose the sex toy according to the area to be stimulated, how and with whom. The choice of a sex toy is extremely personal. So, before you buy a sex toy, you have to do a reconnaissance tour between your most intimate desires and your most hidden fantasies and ask yourself:

- Which area of your body do you want to stimulate: the clitoris? The G-spot? The B side? Or maybe several areas at once?

- How would you like to stimulate this area: there are not only vibrators!

- Who you want to use it with, where and in what situations: it is very important to define the style and size of the sex toy and to be able to take advantage of its services. For example, a rabbit vibrator might be great for solo use, but it might be too bulky if you're looking for something to put in your bag without too much embarrassment.

- Listen to your instinct: there must be some kind of lightning bolt between you and the sex toy that makes you say "yes, you are the one!"

16

*Sex toy: choose by material*
Always be informed about the materials of a sex toy, both for hygienic reasons and for the sensations that the different materials can give. Indeed:

- materials must be safe for health: the best are silicone, steel, borosilicate glass, pyrex, wood (especially ebony) and ceramics, which are easy to clean and sterilize and do not contain toxic substances.
- silicone is a fairly rigid material, but with heat it tends to soften and "adapts" to the body. At the same time, steel, ceramic, borosilicate glass and pyrex are very rigid materials, but give intense sensations and can be cooled or heated at will
- we do not recommend PVC, gelly or cyberskin sex toys, which may contain phthalates, substances harmful to the body that would be easily absorbed by the mucous membranes.

## Sex toys: choose according to price
A sex toy must fit your taste and also your wallet. So ask yourself: *what kind of object do I want and how much do I want to spend?*

As far as style is concerned, we can count: the anatomical-realistic, decidedly explicit, the unsuspected, which hides the erotic function in disguise; the latest generation design, elegant and not too explicit, which reconciles functionality and aesthetics; the ironic, with funny shapes and bright colours; the luxury, with precious and expensive materials.

Prices range from a few dollars (for example, the disposable vibrating ring), to a few thousand in the case of gold or silver dildos and vibrators. Generally speaking, good quality products are affordable but not "for sales": it is often worth investing in a well-made object that you really like, rather than saving money and not being satisfied.

## Sex toys: how they work
The modes and operation are not the same for all sex toys. Here is some useful information:

- Dildos don't vibrate, so they work "by hand" and are silent, vibrators may not.
- Vibrators can have one or more vibration intensities, a "fixed" vibration and/or different vibration paths that combine pulses of different intensities, some can be programmed and even go to music. Needless to say, more possibilities for enjoyment are better than one.
- Some vibrators also produce movements: those of the famous Twist&Shake are circular and particularly suitable to stimulate the G point.
- Vibrators can have different control modes: a wheel, buttons, a remote control with or - better - wireless.
- There are vibrators powered by batteries, rechargeable from the socket and rechargeable via USB port.

17

- Vibrators can: have a curvature to stimulate the G point (even dildos), be specific for the clitoris or the B side, be waterproof or wearable, stimulate multiple erogenous zones simultaneously.

## Tips for use and storage

To fully enjoy the performance of a sex toy, it is advisable to use it with a lubricant (which you can buy with your toy):

- Water-based lubricants are suitable for use with condoms and all materials, but tend to dry out quickly;
- Silicone based lubricants provide more comfort, but are incompatible with condoms and silicone toys, which may deteriorate.
- Sex toys should be cleaned before and after each use, and should be stored carefully, both for hygienic reasons and to avoid damage and deterioration.

To do so, you can use a specific product (you can find them where you buy the toy), disinfectant and hypoallergenic. The silicone, steel, ceramic, glass and pyrex sex toys can also be sterilized with a more homemade but less practical method, i.e. in boiling water.

Sex toys: types to choose from

Finally, here is a short overview that will help you to orient yourself in the universe of sex toys to choose between fun, couple, superhitech etc., for all tastes

- Rabbit type double stimulation vibrator
- Multi-vibration pocket vibrator, suitable for both internal and clitoral stimulation
- Clitoris-specific vibrator
- Unsuspected vibrator: perhaps not the greatest pleasure, but it can also be used on the whole body. There are also "universal" vibrators, with a less fun look, which are suitable both for relaxing back or muscle massages and for intimate massages.
- Wearable clitoral vibrator, butterfly with panties, to stimulate the clitoris: another great classic. There are also pre-op versions for double stimulation or vaginal stimulation
- Dildo with suction cup base: can be attached to surfaces such as walls and floors
- G-spot specific dildo, thanks to its characteristic curvature
- Anal toys: they usually have rounded shapes and are made up of some spheres, they can be vibrating or not. Another example of anal toys is the butt-plug, with the characteristic wedge shape
- Sex toys for men: these are usually masseurs - vibrating or not - for prostate massage, penis rings (12) or "complements" to masturbation
- Sex toys for couples: They stimulate both partners and are suitable to experience some particular erotic situation.

- Geisha balls provide only a slight stimulation, but their virtue is to strengthen the pelvic floor, for longer, easier and more powerful orgasms.
- Whether they vibrate or not, cockrings or penis rings serve to improve and prolong erection and stimulate the clitoris during intercourse.

Below you will find our list of the best Sex Toys, surely you can find the one that suits you best!

## 17 + 1 Sex Toys For Intense Orgasms

No more classic vibrators: the new sex toys are eco-friendly, remote-controlled, rechargeable and innovatively designed! Here's an overview of the latest best in erotic games.

### Ki-Wi
You don't eat it, but it could be forbidden fruit. It's not an animal, but it has an interesting long "nose". Ki-Wi is a stimulator for the Clit, which makes speed its most important feature, very silently tickling the most sensitive parts of the female body. It can also be used in water or the dark, because it is waterproof and glows in the dark... pure pleasure!

### Nobessence
Some would say sex toys are something unnatural. To disprove skeptics and tempt lovers of ecology and renewable materials, the wooden dildos - indeed, the sculptures - produced by Nobessence are ideal. There are dildos in all shapes and for all tastes and if at some point you get tired of them and they don't warm you up anymore... they can be recycled in the fireplace. Although, personally, it would be a waste.

### Zoon +
It is a wireless sex toy that can be used either at short distance with a remote control (for example: in a restaurant, supermarket...) or at thousands of kilometers controlling it from the website, even over oceanic distances.

### Tor
The new jewel in LELO's collection is this vibrant ring, as precious as a solitaire but decidedly more suitable for couples' games, thanks to its two-hour charge (yes, it is rechargeable and not disposable) and its 6 (and I say 6) stimulation modes. After all, there are many ways to say "Yes".

## Ina

Ina is not only a beautiful sex toy, it's a real bomb: a double action vibrator (internal and external) with 2 powerful vibrating motors for 8 different modes. What's new in this little toy with a refined Swedish design is the "circular mode" of the vibrations, which transfers a more intense stimulation first in one sensitive point, then in the other, creating a sensation of internal movement to reach explosive orgasms.

## Squeel

It looks like the propeller of a motorboat, it's actually a sex toy that simulates oral sex thanks to its 10 silicone tabs that give a sea of orgasms. No need to add more.

## Lovemoiselle

This brand new brand produces ceramic sex toys, a very, very interesting material: smooth as silk, it lends itself to pleasant games with temperature, from very cold to very hot. In the picture you can see two dildos, Noemie (pink) and Aveline (blue, which has a curvature to stimulate the G-spot), but there are also vibrators, always in ceramic.

## Eve

An intimate masseur as light as a leaf, silky and elegant, which rests gently on the most sensitive points of the body, but manages to reverse the seasons: when the leaves fall, spring begins...of the senses.

## Form 2

A small clitoral vibrator to hear a powerful stereo pleasure (each "ear" provides intense stimulation) with a compact and elegant sex toy. And water-resistant, for singing in the shower and bathtub. Rechargeable.

## Better Than Chocolate

The name says it all: this clit vibrator is better than chocolate. Simple to use thanks to a user-friendly controller, it dispenses orgasms as if they were chocolates thanks to a very powerful and silent vibration, with different modes and speeds but, unlike chocolate, it doesn't melt in water: it resists up to a meter deep.

## Pure Wand

This pure steel dildo has the curve in the right place to reach all the innermost secrets and make you touch the sky with a finger. And then it's beautiful, it's easy to clean (it's important, before and after each use!), the material is great to play with the temperature and experience very interesting sensations... it's no coincidence that it won an award for best "emerging" sex toy of 2009.

## Bcurious
An ideal name for this small rechargeable vibrator with a very curious shape. It stimulates the clitoris by precisely tracing the contours of the female body to give an intense and silent pleasure. Suitable to act undisturbed in the bathtub (it is waterproof) or anywhere else, with 4 amazing stimulation modes. Not a comma is missing.

## Contour Q
Okay. They're beautiful. But what are they for? They're a pair of porcelain "stones" to perform a modern version of the traditional stone massage. They are enclosed in the palm and slide over the whole body (even with the help of an oil) to release tension, caress sensitive areas and discover some unexpected points of pleasure thanks to the two stimulating surfaces, to be heated or cooled at will. Try it under the soles of your feet.

## Teneo Uno and Duo
The smartballs of Fun Factory - a German company of excellence - are committed to improving the comfort and results of Kegel exercises that strengthen the pelvic floor muscles and improve orgasm. Hence the geisha balls Teneo 1, for beginners, and Teneo 2, for a more advanced level, both carved to give more pleasant sensations and get the most out of training.

## Tickle-Popzzz
These lollipop-shaped vibrators could please Candy Candy, with their soft rubber suitable to pamper the most sensitive points of our body. A sweet pleasure without guilt and without arousing suspicion.

## Kokeshi Dancer
These innocent dolls are actually waterproof massagers with 3 vibration speeds. Perfect to keep on the edge of the bathtub for fun water games, or undisturbed on the bedside table.

## Sexy Bunny
Follow the pink rabbit and the orgasms will be a wonder. This vibrator - in slang "dual action vibe" or "rabbit", just like the one that caused a certain... addiction to Charlotte in Sex & the City - combines clitoral and vaginal stimulation with a fun pink & punk design.

Cry baby

The tears, of course, are dictated by emotion. Here is the prince of vibrating eggs: ten programs and no strings. Just use the remote control to tune into the right frequency... Special for playing in pairs, especially outside the bedroom. Now it's up to you to let your imagination run wild.

# KAMASUTRA – CHAPTER WITH SEX PICTURES POSITIONS

## The Benefits of Kamasutra

It invigorates a connection.

Long-term spouses sometimes find that their relationship becomes stale with time. Experimenting with various positions may spice up a couple. Some classes, such as the Corkscrew and the Carousel, encourage closeness.

It improves a person's sexual pleasure.

Kamasutra isn't only about sex. It considers sex to be more than simply a physical experience. It is a method of achieving fulfillment through pushing one's physical limits. Sex energises the body while also enhancing the immune system? Overall, Kamasutra places a high importance on the sex experience since it allows partners to feel good about themselves both physically and intellectually.

While experience and physical strength can help determine how delightful and practical more advanced sexual positions are, there is one technique for everyone to get physically prepared to try them out. This is also sound advise for folks concerned about their flexibility or having difficulty entering more accessible sexual positions:

Take a yoga class or any other type of exercise that focuses on stretching and strengthening your core muscles. The stronger a person's core muscles are, the better they will be in holding various physical positions and have higher overall physical endurance. The more limber and flexible a person is, the simpler it is to move into and maintain difficult positions.

Additional Practices and Steps to Spice Up Your Sex Life

Some people attempt making love or even starting their foreplay with pornography playing in the background to spice up their sex life. Some couples may begin watching pornography together to increase arousal, while others like to have it on as a guide during foreplay. This approach is not for everyone, but it is a great strategy to attempt if you want to learn more about your spouse's sexual preferences or want to visually convey your sexual preferences to your partner in a thrilling and engaging way.

Another option for couples who wish to improve their sex life is to begin their sexual activities before ever sharing a room. Text messaging and the ability to exchange photographs with cellphones has made this far more convenient than it was in previous decades when technology was inadequate. This method does need some amount of confidence between partners, especially if images, video, or audio recordings are to be shared from one phone to another.

The goal of this game is to get the most out of your foreplay. Some couples begin sending each other filthy text messages as soon as they leave for work in the morning, gradually increasing their sensuality and seductiveness until both parties are ready for physical foreplay and intercourse nearly as soon as they get home that evening. When trying this activity, some safety and security tips for men and women are:

Avoid putting your face in any pictures or videos; do not mention names or specific locations in audio recordings; and do not save any pictures or videos that you or your partner would not want someone accidentally stumbling across or finding if your phone is ever stolen.

If you don't want to get in trouble, don't open video or audio communications at work or in public.

While some people may enjoy the risk (it's possible that the risk is one of the reasons the couple chose this method), if anything were to open unexpectedly or be taken by virtual hackers who could be used against the couple, the dangers would shift from exciting and entertaining to very real and unfortunate.

Advice from an Expert for Couples of All Ages

Never use a dry spell as an excuse to call it quits on a relationship. Intimacy is complicated, relationships are complicated, and there are many elements that can affect someone's ability to become aroused:

Emotional, hormonal, psychological, social, and physical stress are all factors to consider.

Dry spells are common, especially among couples who have been together for a long time. While a medical difficulty is always a possibility, for people who have been cleared by a doctor for concerns with their personal sex life, the remedy can be as simple as altering the routine and trying something new. Any of the concepts, strategies, or activities discussed in this book can be utilized to rekindle a sexual passion (in yourself or your partner).

Other possibilities include going to a sexual supplies store or exploring the internet for sex guidance. Every day, new stores and galleries open to cater to people's sexual desires all over the world, regardless of how weird or unique their inclinations may be. Whatever sexual preferences you and your partner have, it is up to both of you to come to terms and communicate properly in order for your sexual, emotional, and romantic interactions to succeed and be completely satisfying!

## The Kama Sutra Sex Positions

Sex is not cut and dried. A lot of different sexual positions are set out by the Kama Sutra. Going down the list, we will go through various sexual positions that not only give you sexual pleasure but also bring you and your partner on a deep, intimate level closer together. The positions we are going to go over are the following:

## Standing Positions

### *The Fan*

Standing, with her knees tight on the edges of a chair and her arms crossed on the back, the woman gives her back to the partner who first brings her to him by insinuating her hands between her slightly spread thighs to stimulate her clitoris, then penetrates her from behind. This position - suitable for both anal and vaginal coitus - allows excellent stress on the woman's vaginal walls and G-spot. Man can also caress her clitoris or breasts before and during penetration.

### _The Padlock_
On the table, on the desk, on the washing machine: the position of the padlock is versatile and guarantees magnetic contact between the two bodies ... The woman is on a high cabinet (a desk, a table, the washing machine), sitting cross-legged and resting on the arms, positioned behind. The man stands in front of her, and the woman crosses her legs behind him, at her sides. He stares at her as the movement begins.

### Luxurious Climb
The couple stands face to face next to the bed. She puts one leg over the bed while the man kneels until he can put her leg over his shoulder. She hugs him around the neck so she can relax and let herself go backwards as the man slowly gets up to penetrate her. She stretches her leg and stretches it to the maximum while he continues with his constant movements.

### The Royal Stairs
The woman kneels on the lowest step of the staircase and leans on an upper step or on the railing. The man takes her by the hips and penetrates her from behind. This position can also be used for anal sex.

### *Standing on a wall*

The man has his back against the wall and penetrates the partner holding her by the thighs and moving the pelvis back and forth to modulate the oscillation of the back and forth.

### The visit

Suitable for any place and circumstance, this position has the flavor of a surprise encounter. Standing, facing each other, the man stimulates with his own sex that of the partner until he reaches a superficial penetration.

To obtain maximum success, it is therefore advisable for the woman to increase her stature by wearing high-heeled shoes or climbing onto any other available support.

### Let it Go

The woman is lying on her back on a pillow with her knees bent. The partner is sitting with her legs under her thighs leans forward to kiss her belly, then lifts the pelvis to penetrate. The man begins to move rhythmically when the woman is abandoned.

### The butterfly

She stretches out on a fairly tall and comfortable piece of furniture, he stands in front of her and takes the partner's legs leaning them over his shoulders. She lifts her arms up raising her pelvis while he helps her by pushing her butt upwards. By maintaining this position he will be able to move inside her at the perfect angle to orgasm.

### The position of the butterfly in practice

While requiring a certain skill, the position of the Butterfly must not be frightening as the two bodies tend to support each other, as long as the right angle is found. First of all, you will have to put yourself on a piece of furniture in which its basin is lower than yours: a table, a desk, the washing machine, the dishwasher ... but it will also depend on how tall you are. The moment you lift your pelvis, your back must form a straight line with its pelvis. In this way, your pubis and his will fit together and he will be able to penetrate you perfectly and without making excessive efforts. To avoid arching your back you will need to ask your partner to support your pelvis with his hands. But you will see that it will be natural for him to do so in order to move more easily.

### A stimulating position

If you feel comfortable in this position (maybe because you do yoga every day or because you have good abdominals), you can use one hand to stroke your breast or masturbate. You will see that your partner will become even more excited seeing that you caress yourself under his eyes. A variant of the classic position in which the man lifts his partner's pelvis to improve the angle of penetration, the butterfly position is original not only because the woman is in an unusual position, but above all because it is practiced outside the bed. And this is already enough to break the routine and make the situation more exciting for both.

### An exclusive orgasm

The Butterfly position is a position that is worth trying also because it promotes vaginal orgasm. In fact in the Butterfly the penetration is deep but it is not parallel to the vaginal canal, as for example in the Missionary position. In doing so, the stimulated area is not the bottom of the vagina, but the anterior part, therefore the G point. The resulting orgasm is strong and makes all the senses vibrate! To add a note of pleasant sensuality to the situation you can also focus on the details: red flowers, candles, incense sticks, two glasses of champagne, romantic background music. With a little imagination, the play between the bodies will be even more intense and spicy.

### The Bracket
The woman is stretched out with her belly up, and her buttocks on the edge of the bed. The man is standing and penetrating her stroking her breasts and clitoris. This position can also be done while standing still. In this case, the woman hugs her partner by crossing her legs. It is very exciting: the woman feels the pulsations of the penis and the man those of the vagina.

### Special chair
The woman sits on him giving him his shoulders and using his arms as a support, he penetrates her from behind and helps her move until the pleasure is achieved.

### The Mermaid
She has to lie down on a table, a bed, or a desk, placing a pillow under her buttocks which must be slightly raised. Then always the woman must raise her legs up, keeping them together. The woman can put her hands under the pillow to give a little more elevation to the pelvis. He performs the penetration while she has her legs up; if the bed or table is low, the man should bend his knees or kneel on the ground. In addition, he can grab his feet to leverage, so as to be more stable if he wants to push deeper.

## Scissors

She is lying supine on a table, with her pelvis at the edge and stretching her legs upwards. The man is standing in front of her and holds her by the ankles penetrating her. In making the move, the man continues to open and close the woman's legs, mimicking scissors.

Let yourself be tempted by the unique sensations of bondage. If you like having sex on your feet this is the position for you! If you don't feel like dominating, let yourself be carried away by the impetus of your him.

## The Climb

The man is firmly on his feet and lifts the woman who is standing before him. She wraps it with her legs, keeping her feet on a bed or sofa. The man makes the woman go up and down, trying to produce a movement from top to bottom while maintaining the same speed and depth.

## Sexy 5

The woman must sit on a piece of furniture or a table and the man must stand in front of her. His legs must be slightly bent, spaced about 90 cm apart. The woman rests the arms on the man, who instead has his arms around the lower part of her torso. Slowly the woman has to push her left leg up and support her right foot on the man's left shoulder. Do the same thing with the right leg on the man's left shoulder.

### The Hanging Woman
The man lifts the woman holding her under the buttocks. The woman wraps her legs around his hips to hold on and rests her feet against the wall to which the man has to lean.

### Right in target
What you need are a chair, a lot of agility and a good physical shape. She is astride the back of the chair with her torso bent and her elbows resting on her knees.

He holds her by the hips by modulating the swing of the back and forth to achieve maximum excitement.

### The Apple
The man is standing and holding his partner in his arms, supporting her by the buttocks and the back while she wraps him tightly with the legs. The woman can also lean with her back against the wall, so as to have secure support and allow greater penetration. This position has the advantage of being practicable in any place but also has the limitation of being suitable only for a muscular man and of not being able to be maintained for a long time.

### *Standing up*

Standing, skin against skin, she turns her back on him while he, embracing her with passion, brings her to him and penetrates her from behind. To keep her balance better, the woman can lean against the wall or at a table.

## Relaxing and Cuddling Positions
### *The French*
In this Kamasutra position, the man and the woman are lying on their sides. Her buttocks adhere to the partner's pelvis which gently penetrates her. A position that recalls the position of the newborn baby in the womb, the French position instinctively inspires affection and sweetness.

The advantages of the French position

The French position has numerous points in its favor: easy to put into practice, it does not require athlete skills for its execution. It is very relaxing and will allow you to have sex even if you are tired and think (especially him!) Of not being able to do it! Before penetration, you can caress your partner's member with your body. Then, during intercourse, he will be able to caress your clitoris and cover you with kisses and caresses.

This particularly comfortable position is also suitable for pregnant women who do not want to give up the pleasure of sex. Last but not least, the French position is recommended for women who want to become mothers, since by promoting deep penetration, it facilitates the rise of spermatozoa to the uterus. The only drawback of this position (if you can say so) is that, by turning your back on your partner, you cannot look him in the eye.

But the contact between the bodies is such that you can still perceive all its vibrations. And then, to add a further note of romance to the atmosphere, you can decorate the bedroom with roses and candles and put a soft light.

### *The Vertical Hug*
The man lies on his stomach, keeping his legs slightly apart. The woman lies on him on his stomach, letting herself be penetrated and stretching her legs until they are completely extended in the middle of his legs. It is an excellent position for constant contact between partners and for shallow penetration.

## Simplicity

She is lying on her back with her legs spread as he penetrates her. The hands remain free to exchange caresses and effusions. Especially those of the woman, who can passionately caress the man's back and buttocks. A position to make love in all simplicity.

### *Front and back*
She, lying in a supine position, folds her thighs on her belly and rests her feet on the partner's shoulders. Kneeling on her the man penetrates her deeply. This position can provide enormous pleasure to the woman, especially during ejaculation, provided that the vagina is sufficiently lubricated to prevent the particularly intense penetration from being painful.

### The bell

the woman is bent forward and the man penetrates her while sitting semi-seated. Taking hold of her feet, she moves slowly as he covers her back with kisses. It is a position that requires agility but that allows you to rediscover often forgotten corners of your partner's body.

## Crisscross

The woman lies down on one side with her arms above her head. The man has to stand perpendicular on the woman's side, and slowly the woman has to lift her left leg and make the man put his lower body between his legs.Once she is well united, the woman must grab the man by the shoulders while anchored on the floor.

### Siesta in couple

We suggest this position as a relaxing stop during your "love marathon". You will enjoy a sweet doing nothing made of looks and caresses. Even your body will benefit from the drop in pressure, recommended before resuming more demanding erotic games.

### The Laying Char

The man leans on his hands. The partner reclines comfortably on some pillow with her legs resting on the man's shoulders and moves rhythmically. This position allows a deep penetration and causes a very intense pleasure.

### Orient secrets

He is straight on his knees while the woman, in a supine position and with her legs bent, rests her feet against his chest. The man can bend backward or forwards, thus moving away or bringing the partner's thighs closer to his breast. This position allows very deep penetration.

### *Passionate Proposal*

The position of the passionate proposal requires a little practice and a lot of will. Kneeling face to face, the man puts his foot firmly planted on the ground in front of him (as if he were making a marriage proposal) and the woman puts her right foot on the ground, climbing over his kneeling leg.

The penetration can be done by leaning forward towards the planted feet, making lunges, as if you were dancing slow.

### The pinwheel

The woman and the man are lying facing each other. The woman must bring her groin closer to hers, wrapping her legs around the sides of her torso. Her arms must be extended behind to support the weight. He surrounds the woman's waist with his legs and holds her thighs, gently pushing.

### The sandwich

The woman stretches out on the man, spreads her legs apart to facilitate penetration, and immediately closes them so that the two bodies are perfectly superimposed. He then begins to stimulate his partner by rubbing his own body against that of his partner laterally and horizontally. It is a very intimate position that allows maximum physical contact and satisfies minute women who usually prefer to be on top.

### The Lazy 2

The man kneels with his buttocks resting on his heels and supports himself with his arms. The woman is lying on the bed with her head on the pillow and her back well stretched out. To allow optimal penetration, raise your partner's tight thighs. It can stimulate other areas by dispensing stroking the breasts and the mount of Venus. Particularly sexy and exciting, this position offers deep penetration and offers partners the opportunity to observe each other.

# Bonding

### *The Lazy Man*
The man is lying with his legs dangling at the edges of the bed and his feet on the ground while the woman, resting on him, keeps her thighs wide apart to allow the partner to stimulate her clitoris and she to caress the base of the penis. To increase penetration, she moves rhythmically, gripping her knees. This position offers the man a particularly exciting view of his partner's penetration, buttocks, and sex. Taking advantage of the free hands, it can also stimulate the anal area and the buttocks.

### *The ascendant*

The man and the woman are facing each other on their knees. He tucks his thighs into hers. This particularly intimate position allows the two lovers to embrace, kiss, caress in a swirling interweaving of passion and desire.

### The Joint
The man and the woman are lying side by side in a fetal position. The woman sticks her pelvis to that of her partner and crosses her legs. The man caresses the woman's clitoris during intercourse. Before penetration, the woman can caress the member of her partner with her body. This position proves to be very stimulating if accompanied by caresses.


### The Confession
The man sneaks gently between the partner's legs. She is lying on her side with her knees bent, her feet crossed and she squeezes him tightly with her legs. During the penetration, he can caress his sex and the back of his neck. Taking advantage of this position made of intimacy and sweetness, the two lovers can share pleasures and desires to be discovered together.


### Don't Go
The man is lying on his side. The woman lies down next to him with her head at the height of the feet and squeezes his pelvis with her thighs raised rubbing it with her breasts. Particularly excited from the point of view, during penetration he can caress her buttocks and gently insert his fingers into the anus, a highly erogenous zone.

## Zen

This position is ideal for taking a breather between more complex positions that require more "work". The man and the woman are lying on their sides looking at each other and the legs are crossed one to the other to facilitate penetration. The movements must be practically in unison and can be alternated between slow and faster until orgasm is reached.

## Woman Dominates Positions

### The Spanish

In this position, the man rests one hand on the ground and sits with his legs stretched out while the woman, on her back, kneels astride him and moves rhythmically. In the Spanish position, it is the woman who has an active role, even if in any case the partner can swing the back of her partner and therefore intervene in the rhythm of the penetration, thanks to the hand that is free. Moreover, to make the position even more exciting, the partner can caress her partner's breasts, buttocks, and clitoris while taking advantage of a splendid view of her lower back!

### A voluptuous position

Easy to perform position, both for him and for her, the Spanish position guarantees deep penetration and strong sensations for both partners. If you like being on top and amaze your partner, this position is made for you! Of course, you won't have to be afraid to show your B side, and if you think your partner can see your little flaws, know that he won't even notice! If you are a romantic girl and you don't want to be able to look into your eyes Comrade, you could overcome this inconvenience by creating an erotic atmosphere: rose petals, background music, soft lights, a glass of sparkling wine ... each of these details will add a note of sensuality to the situation. Or, simply stand in front of a mirror and look at each other in this unusual way and for this reason even more exciting!

The Spanish position can be considered a variant of the famous position of the doggie. Deep penetration, the possibility of wide and slow movements: the two positions have many advantages in common, with the difference that in the Spanish position the man is sitting on the ground and therefore the woman is in command.

### *Back View*
On the bed, the man is seated and his legs are stretched out horizontally. The woman must creep under her legs in a rear position and help penetration. The woman then has to stretch her legs, trying to put them behind him, and relax her torso between his feet. The woman must then slide up and down using his feet to leverage.

### *Riding Backwards*
The man is lying on his back. The woman is astride him backward. The woman can caress the partner or the clitoris by moistening her fingers with saliva or vaginal secretions.

### Sitting face to tits

The man is seated on the ground or on the bed with one elongated leg and the other slightly bent to feel well in balance. The woman reclines on him astride rising and sitting rhythmically while the partner supports her by the buttocks. The man can also stimulate his partner's breasts with kisses and pacifiers or have fun nibbling her nipples.

### The Amazon

Mythical position of the Kamasutra, the Amazon is also among the most practiced and appreciated by women. Why? We will explain it to you right away ...

But first of all, what is the origin of the name of this position? You must know that in ancient times the Amazons were a people of female warriors. Between myth and reality, these women have made a lot of talk about them, provoking numerous erotic fantasies. Vestige of this legend in which women take power over men, in the position of the Amazon the woman becomes the architect of her pleasure and dominates the man by placing herself on him, like a rider on his horse. Practiced since ancient times, the position of the Amazon is also known as the "position of Andromache". In fact, the wife of Hector, the hero of Homer's Iliad, used to practice this position.

### The position of the rider in practice

Going to the point, in this position the man is lying on his back with his legs close together. The woman reclines on him and begins to ride him, moving the body according to the movement and inclination that she prefers. To vary the rhythm and depth of the penetration, you can use your feet as support or bring your torso backward using your arms.

A comfortable position for both and easy to practice, in the Amazon you are in charge, while the man, immobilized by your body, is lulled by the rhythmic movements that you perform and has his hands free to stimulate your breast and clitoris.

### Intense pleasure for her

If women like Amazon so much, there is a reason, and this is that this position promotes vaginal orgasm. In fact, in order for a position to favor female pleasure, the penis must stimulate the G-spot area, rather than the bottom of the vagina, such as in the missionary position. In the Amazon of the Kamasutra the two partners are facing each other and the penetration is a little bias and deep. The anterior area of the vagina is therefore stressed by movements, making this position particularly conducive to stimulating the G-spot and therefore to the female orgasm. Here is revealed the secret of the Amazon's position!

### And for him?

47

So, all selfish women who practice or who want to try this Kamasutra position? Not really, as much as the Amazon gives him intense pleasure. Comfortably relaxed, your partner can let go and take full advantage of the sensations brought about by your movements. For him, the vision of your body moving on him will be very stimulating and he will be able to participate in the action by caressing you.

### A location for all occasions

Sensual and exciting position for both partners, the Amazon can also be practiced sitting and dressed. In short, when desire makes itself felt, there is always a way to satisfy it thanks to this position!

Another advantage of the Amazon is that being the woman to dictate the rhythm of the movements, male pleasure increases more progressively: it will therefore be a position to be privileged if your him tends to ejaculate quickly.

To vary ...

The position of the Amazon is also practical because it can be performed in many different ways: from lying down, sitting, on a chair, on the bed, on the sofa. Furthermore, if you want to offer your partner the vision of your lower back, you can try the position of the Viking Ride, in which the woman sits astride the partner and gives him her back. The man holds it by the high end of the thighs, modulating if he wishes, the oscillation of the back and forth. And since the eyes also want their part, in this position your man will have a heavenly vision of your B side!

### The Sofa

The man is sitting on a sofa or chair, with his back resting. His feet must be resting on the ground. The woman sits on the man, facing him. The woman then moves the upper body downwards, backward, resting it on his thighs, and placing her hands backward, on the floor to keep herself. Then he opens and closes his legs to get into the rhythm.

### The English Mount

He lies on his back keeping his legs slightly apart and his head resting on the pillow. She leans on him sideways, with the legs on one side and the rest of the body on the other, keeping his legs well closed and leaning on the arms for better support. At the moment of penetration, she opens her legs slightly and begins to make circular, slow, and continuous movements, alternating with vertical movements. To facilitate orgasm, the man can carry out movements equal and opposite to those of the woman.

### The tarantula

The man is resting on his hands, the legs are stretched on the bed. The woman is astride him and rests her hands next to his legs. The woman goes back and forth rhythmically with the pelvis.

### Bite her Hairs
The man is lying on his back. She is lying on him resting on her elbows, with semi-flexed legs. The man penetrates the partner holding her for life. The woman lifts her pelvis then leans it against him.

### Hot Rubbing
Leaning on one arm, the man is seated on his side and holds one knee on the ground. Leveraging his forearms and giving him his shoulders, the woman rubs on her sex and moves rhythmically to facilitate penetration. With his free hand, he can also caress her breasts, buttocks, and anal area. It is advisable to practice this position on a carpet rather than on the bed.

### The Viking ride
The woman leans back to her partner and reclines around him. The man holds her by the high end of the thighs and modulates the oscillation of the back and forth. This position allows the woman to caress the partner's scrotum, while the man can appreciate the partner's buttocks up close. It is an easy position to perform especially for the partner, who is pleasantly seated. It is also a comfortable position for men, as it is relaxed and has a beautiful view!

Furthermore, if you are a girl who does not like positions in which the woman has a passive role, know that this position is made for you as it is not said that the man controls movements, indeed! In fact, if it is the man who modulates the oscillation, it is the woman who guides the penetration, moving the body according to the movement and inclination that it wants. You can place your hands onman's legs and you can tilt yourself back forward or backward, to change the angle of penetration. In short, in this position neither the man nor the woman controls, and the greater the complicity between the partners, the more coordinated the movements and the better the sensations experienced by both.

This position allows the woman to caress the man's genitals and the man, in turn, to caress the woman's back. In fact, if he lets the woman guide the movements, the man will have his hands completely free and he will also be able to appreciate the partner's B side closely!

### An exciting position for both

Highly erotic position, we can consider this position as a variant of Amazon's position, as in this case too the woman is sitting astride the partner, albeit from her back. The Viking ride is a position that facilitates vaginal orgasm in how much you can control the penetration and then find the angle that allows you to experience greater pleasure. The clitoris is also stimulated by rubbing, and if you feel comfortable in this position it may also masturbate while you move.

For men, this position is very exciting as it can completely let go and feel the pleasure growing. However, some men do not appreciate this position because subjected to the rhythm of their partner, they do not have total control of their pleasure, and they feel destabilized by this situation.

### To feel at ease ...

You too may be reluctant to try this position as you cannot look your partner in the eye, but only perceive his reactions from his moans and movements. Furthermore, knowing that your partner can observe your back and his small defects at will (even if, of course, your partner misses it), you may feel uncomfortable. But the solution exists: why don't you offer your man to blindfold himself? Doing so would better savor your every move! Furthermore, since the position does not allow you to exchange languid looks looking into your eyes, you can enhance the romantic atmosphere by decorating the bedroom with roses and candles, lowering the light, and putting a little background music. To have eye contact with your partner, you can easily alternate this position and the position of the Amazon. In short, the tricks exist to make this position not only very conducive to orgasm but also very sensual!

### The Steamer
He is lying on his back. She sits on her sex with her legs on her side and her thighs spread apart and move rhythmically. The woman can increase the pleasure of deep penetration by caressing herself.

## Man Dominates Positions

### *Doggy Style*

The woman stands on all fours, holding her arms out in front of her head. To maintain balance, the woman shifts the weight onto her hands, keeping her head down. The man kneels behind the woman, holding her hips. The position, also called doggy style, is one of the classics of the Kama Sutra.

### *Legs on shoulder*

She lies down with a pillow under her head and legs in the air as straight and as high as possible. The man is on his knees in front of her, taking her legs and resting them on one shoulder. Pushing forward, he penetrates her, wanting to use the bed or the floor as support by leaning with the other arm.

### *Slipping*

The woman is lying on her stomach on the bed or on the floor, with her legs stretched out and slightly apart. The man sits behind her and arches his body to facilitate penetration, holding onto his arms and resting his hands on the sides of her legs. To intensify the sensations, the woman may slightly close her legs. For convenience, it is recommended that the woman leaning on her elbows.

### *The Candle*

The woman is lying on her back with her legs vertical. The partner, kneeling on the bed or on the ground, lifts her pelvis and penetrates her caressing the lower part of her thighs, a particularly erogenous zone.

The position of the candle in practice

To be more comfortable, the woman can put a pillow under her head and possibly also under her back, so as not to strain the lower back too much. The position of the Candle is in fact a rather acrobatic position for the woman: it, therefore, requires a good physical shape and therefore well-trained abdominal muscles! If you are not very trained, you can still ask your partner to help you lift your pelvis with his hands. To maintain the position more easily, your partner can tighten your pelvis between his thighs. Of course, if you practice yoga for yourself this position will be a breeze!

An exciting location

The advantage of the position of the Candle is that your partner has his hands free to caress not only your thighs but also your clitoris. But you too, if you feel comfortable in this position, you could masturbate while your partner penetrates, making the game even more exciting, both for you and him because he certainly will not mind watching you while you caress ... Also during the action you can exchange glances and sweet or fiery words.

To add a spicy and sensual note to the situation you can ask your partner to blindfold you. This way you can take advantage of every sensation without worrying about what's going on around you. You can decorate the room with roses and candles or put two glasses of sparkling wine in plain sight on a handy tray ...

The position of the candle is interesting because it allows you to have sex by stimulating new muscles and new parts of the body. The sensations change and the senses awaken, especially if in recent times you have always made love in the same position.

An exceptional experience for fans of clitoral orgasm If you don't want to dominate, let yourself be carried away by the impetus of your him Guaranteed orgasm An excellent position if he has a small penis Pamper your G-spot, you won't regret it!

### *The Eight*

The woman is lying on her back, with her legs slightly open, possibly with a pillow under her back to facilitate penetration. The man is lying on the woman and has his hands on one side and the other of her head, with his arms stretched out as if doing the push-ups. The woman holds her hands on the man's hips and helps him form "8" numbers with the hips while he is inside her. The 8 "relaxed" is the symbol of infinity, and it seems like a good promise to be made in two!

## *Flexuosity*

The woman has her knees bent on her belly while the man, kneeling, penetrates her by leaning on one hand and holding the partner's thighs with the other. By taking advantage of the hands-free, she can caress the base of the penis.

Even if it needs good agility, this position allows deep penetration and favors fertilization.

### The Star
The woman is lying on her back, one leg stretched out, the other bent. The man is above her, passes one leg under her raised his thigh, and leans on his elbows. This position is very stimulating: the woman can caress her own body and that of her partner throughout the duration of the intercourse.

### *Bandoleer*

The woman is lying on her back with her legs raised and her knees joined against her chest, the man kneels and penetrates her. In this position, the G-spot is stimulated more intensely.

### Samba

The woman is lying on her side on the bed or on the floor, with her legs stretched out at an angle of ninety degrees (L-shaped). He is lying behind her penetrating her as he raises his torso with his arms, placing his hand higher on the opposite side of his body next to his chest and turning around a bit. It is the man who controls all the movement.

### *Look me in the eye*

Here is a variant of the missionary's classic and universally appreciated position. The woman is lying with her thighs apart and a few pillows under her buttocks to optimize the angle of penetration. The man reclines between his legs and leans on his forearms to better modulate the oscillation of back and forth. This position, at the same time stimulating and relaxing, allows the couple to look at each other, kiss, and embrace each other despite limits the freedom of movement of the woman, proving to be sometimes boring.

## The Lateral Join
With her back to her partner lies down on her side. The man kneels behind the woman so that the two bodies are perpendicular. The man takes the woman's lower leg and moves it while penetrating her. She takes her upper leg and stretches it slightly to give him better visibility. To get used to the push he can hold the woman by the hips.

## The Let's go home
Clinging to your partner, the Let's go home position will make you live a romantic and exciting moment.

In this position the woman is lying on her stomach, even better if with a pillow under the buttocks to slightly raise the pelvis. The woman moves her hips while he penetrates her. It is a perfect location after a romantic dinner because it also helps digestion.

## Dirty Dance
She lies down on a rigid surface, like the floor, faces upwards, and bends her knees on her belly, keeping her arms stretched along the surface, above her head.

He stands over her with his legs straight and outstretched and his arms stretched over his partner's shoulders. In this way, he penetrates her and controls the movement with large circular movements or with strong rhythmic pushes, as she likes more.

## The Sphinx
The woman leans on her arms with a bent leg. The man above her moves rhythmically.

## Adoration
She is crawling, resting comfortably on her elbows. He keeps with his knees bent, embraces her, and penetrates her from behind. This classic position is pleasant for both. In fact, the deep penetration stimulates the vagina and the G-spot a lot and the partner can caress the clitoris and breasts. Very exciting for him, who with this position can satisfy his desire to dominate women. However, some women feel humiliated in this position, while others find it particularly painful.

## Nirvana
The woman is lying on her back, with her legs stretched out and her arms above her head. The man is lying on top of her. As the man slides inside the woman, she keeps all the muscles in tension, tightens her legs, and pushes her arms against the bed. This will increase the penetration space and allow a natural stimulation of the clitoris.

### *Lotus*
Lying on her back, the woman crosses her legs on her chest. The man is above her and penetrates her. If desired, a cushion can be used to slightly change the angle of penetration. In order not to weigh too much on the woman, the man can alternate the support of his weight between her legs and his wrists, while the woman can increase the excitement by using her hands to caress her partner.

### Indrani

The woman is lying on her back, with her knees against her chest. The man kneels and penetrates her. For deeper penetration, the woman can place her hands on his buttocks and pull him towards her, keeping her feet resting on his chest.

### *Utphallaka*

The man kneels on the bed. The woman lies down on her back, raises her buttocks, and wraps her legs around him.

As the man penetrates her, the woman arches her back, getting help from him, who holds her hands under her back.

### *The Magical Mountain*

First of all, build your mountain of pillows. The woman is kneeling in front of the pillows. The man is kneeling behind her, with his legs outside hers. He lies down with his torso on her and penetrates from behind. Be sure to use fairly firm cushions to create the mountain.

### Odalisque
The woman is stretched out with her legs spread and her knees bent. He remains motionless while the man, seated between her thighs, gently lifts her pelvis to penetrate her and kiss her belly. A position loved by those women who willingly give up taking the initiative.

### The Gold Triangle
At first glance, the position of the Golden Triangle recalls the classic missionary position: the woman lying down with the man on top. However, the trick of this position is that the man has to crawl and the woman lifts her pelvis towards the penis to get penetrated. He remains in this position while the woman does all the work.

## Sitting positions

### Lotus
The male sits with his legs crossed while the lady sits on top of him. He rhythms the movement with his hands and caresses the partner's breast with his mouth.

### *The Magical Ride*
The man is sitting comfortably in a chair and the woman is leaning against him. As she moves, he nibbles on her breast.

### Rocking horse

In the position of the rocking horse, the woman dominates the partner, holding on tightly to him. A sensual and very exciting position for both of them... The man sits cross-legged, holding his hands on the back. The woman sits on the man, with her face turned towards him, wrapping him with her legs.

The man sits cross-legged, keeping his hands on the back. The woman sits on the man, with her face turned towards him, wrapping him with her legs. The woman can thus decide the rhythm and depth of penetration. To free his arms and caress the woman, the man could lean his back against a wall, thus having his hands free.

### The Rocking Chair

Stand astride your man, so that you are face to face. Once it's inside you, wrap your legs around his buttocks and make him do the same. Then you and your man should join your elbows under each other's knees and lift them up to the level of the chest. Then start rocking with forward-backward movements.

### The love chair

He is sitting on a chair. The partner, resting on her legs, moves rhythmically, rising and sitting down. The man can stimulate her clitoris while she caresses her breasts.

### The Lazy Mermaid

The man is seated. She sits astride him, throws herself back, and rests her head on a pillow. The man moves rhythmically and caresses her breasts. This position requires great agility.

### The Limbo

He sits in a rather comfortable chair with a cushion resting under his knees to keep them slightly raised. She sits astride, lowering himself on him and raising his legs on his shoulders. He hugs her to help her move and keep her in balance. Once the man has penetrated her, the woman starts to move pushing her legs towards the back of the chair while he pushes upwards.

### The naughty

Sit both on the bed and let yourself be carried away by a particularly pleasant Kamasutra position: the Naughty!

The man is seated on the edge of the bed with his feet on the ground and his back straight. With her back to her, she reclines on her sex and modulates the swing of the back and forth clinging to the partner's hands and legs. He can accompany the movement by lifting her buttocks.

Pressed against each other, the position of the Naughty will allow you to exchange effusions and sweet words. It is a pleasant position for both partners because the angle that the woman's pelvis assumes allows particularly deep penetration. Furthermore, both the man and the woman are in charge of the pushes' rhythm and intensity. And to finish while you move, your partner will be able to caress your clitoris and breasts.

The only drawback of this position, if we can say so, is that the Naughty does not allow to look straight in the eye. But the closeness and the contact between the bodies still allows to exchange heat and sensations, and, for the woman, to feel protected by the body of the partner. So if you have a romantic soul, this

position is made for you! And if you really feel frustrated because the eye wants its part and you cannot exchange languid looks with your partner, you can still create a sensual atmosphere by decorating the bedroom with rose petals and candles, putting some background music and burning an incense stick, just like the aristocratic Indian couples would have done, to whom the author of the original Kamasutra addressed with his book about love and eroticism, which later became famous all over the world.

## Acrobatic positions

### *The Y*

She lies on the bed belly down making her body protrude, from the pelvis down, beyond the bed, resting her hands on the floor to support the weight. He positions himself above her, his legs between those of her. He penetrates her from behind. The man can also take the woman by the hips and lift her back instead of lying on top of her.

### The X

This position is all about control: your man is lying on his back on the bed. Turn around and straddle above him, so that your back is towards him, and then lower yourself onto his erect penis. Extend her legs back towards her shoulders and bring your torso towards the bed, between her legs. With both your legs and your man's legs you will form an X. Then start sliding up and down. To get more thrust use his feet.

### Alternating legs

The woman is resting on her back with one leg on the shoulder of her boyfriend. He penetrates her while on his knees, gripping the ankle of her straight leg in one hand and the knee with the other. By taking advantage of the free hands, the woman can caress her breasts or stimulate the sex of her partner. A variant may be to repeat the same movement with the other leg and so on alternating them.

### The boat

Kneeling at the bed's edge, the guy penetrates his companion, who is laying on his back. Holding her by the ankles, she slightly raises her legs apart and moves rhythmically. The penetration is very deep, relaxing for her, and particularly exciting for him, which dominates the situation from above. Depending on the stature of the man, it may be necessary to use a cushion to lift the partner's buttocks.

### The Drawbridge

Among the most acrobatic positions of the Kamasutra, there is certainly that of the Drawbridge.

As the name of the position itself says, the man must form a bridge with the body, while the woman leans against him and let herself be penetrated. Pubis versus pubis, it's a great position if you prefer the rotational movements of the pelvis rather than the classic up and down. This position can only be performed if your partner is strong and trained and has no back problems. It is also a position that requires a lot of balance. He may also try to raise and lower the pelvis, but the movement will be limited by your body.

This is a very pleasant position as the penetration is deep and the contact between your pubis is very exciting for the clitoris! While he is moving, you can caress his chest or, by moving one arm backwards, you can gently stimulate the area of the inner thighs, but avoid tickling him, so as not to lose his balance. To be able to relax even more and not have to stay on tiptoe, especially if he is big and you are small, try to wear high heels: in this way maintaining the position will be less tiring, both for you and for him, you will have more stability, and you can focus on your feelings.

To add a spicy and sensual note to this position, you can blindfold yourself, to better savor every movement. Also, in order not to have the feeling of being at a gymnastics course, you can create a romantic atmosphere by decorating the room or bedroom with roses and candles ... If you feel inspired by the position of the drawbridge, know that there is one a female variant, in which it is the woman who stands below and arches her body in such a way as to have her pubis well exposed, while the man penetrates her standing on it, with her legs slightly bent, and avoiding sitting on top of her partner, not to drop it.

Among the positions of the Kamasutra that look like this and that you may want to try is that of the Monkey, in which the man lies down and collects his legs in the chest. Then the woman sits on him and lets her partner put her feet on her back. In this case, it is the woman who guides the movements and the depth of the penetration.

There are many positions in the Kamasutra, and you are spoiled for choice! And the more you try, the more you will want to make them yours by adding detail, a certain way of caressing or moving, particular lingerie, or maybe a sex toy. The variations are infinite, as infinite as the imagination!

### The Triumph Arc
Your man is sitting on the bed with his legs stretched out in front of him. Get on your knees above him, lowering yourself on his erect penis. Once you are comfortable, arch your back, but be careful not to strain the lower back. Place your head between your legs on the bed and grab your ankles or feet. At that moment he can bend forward and the fun can begin.

### Propeller
In a conventional missionary position, the guy is laying on top of the lady. While above the woman, maintaining the position gives the momentum to make a 360 degree rotation. To help him, the woman must guide him with her body, like the propeller over a helicopter, making sure to lift his legs when they swing overhead.

### _The Indian Headstand_

The woman is resting on her hands, her arms are stretched out. The man is at the edge of the bed and lifts her pelvis, while she rests her legs on the partner's arms. It is a position that requires great agility, a little strength and that cannot last more than a few minutes.

### *Supernova*

The Supernova begins with the classic position with the woman on top of the man, standing on the covers. The man must have his head on the side of the bottom of the bed. She crouches on him with her knees bent and feet well placed on the bed as he penetrates her.

The woman bends backward leaning on her arms and moves until orgasm is reached. When the time comes she throws herself forward towards the man and leaning on her knees, she pushes the man towards the edge of the bed until she protrudes until her shoulders and arms are completely outside the pallet. At this point, the woman moves to the starting position until the pleasure for both is achieved.

### The monkey

The man lies down and collects his legs in the chest. The woman sits on him and lets her partner put her feet on her back. For more intense stimulation and to help balance, the partners can support each other by holding their wrists.

### Gravity

The woman is resting on her back with her legs drawn up to her sternum. He is kneeling in front of the woman, holding his feet. With just the movement of the hips, the man can penetrate her while controlling the movement and helps to keep her in balance. To increase the pleasure she can put her feet on his chest, holding her hips still further giving him extra control and letting him penetrate even more.

### The Head Game

start this game by placing yourself face down, face down. With your hands hold on to the lower back and raise your legs and back, so that it is as perpendicular as possible. At this point, your man kneels in front of you, grabs your ankles, and puts his knees at the height of your shoulders. Then grab his hands and ask him to hold you by the hips. You will both be stronger. Hold her thigh to leverage and get her genitals to enjoy an otherworldly experience.

### Pinball

The woman is lying on her stomach. The man is kneeling in front of her, grabs her pelvis, and keeps him at the height of the penis. This position leads to excitement very quickly. For a more comfortable variant, the man is seated on his heels, he draws the partner's pelvis to himself, stroking her clitoris.

### The Clamp

This position is decidedly complex and requires good musculature for both, particularly for the woman's arms. The woman lies on her side, rising with her left arm and keeping her calves, feet, and ankles on the mattress. The man supports her by holding her by the pelvis and, lifting her right leg, penetrates her. Despite being very difficult to perform, it is a position that promises deep penetration and explosive orgasm.

### *The wheelbarrow*

In this position, the woman stands before the man, who takes her ankles. The woman folds her legs, bringing her knees close to her chest, and leans her legs against his. The man then penetrates her from behind. An acrobatic position especially for the woman, the wheelbarrow requires a lot of physical endurance and therefore, for both, arms and abdominal muscles well trained! But contrary to appearances, the bulk of the effort is not up to you but him: you will only have to keep your balance, while he, in addition to penetrating you, will also have to support your weight, without letting you fall. A real challenge to gravity!

To make the position more comfortable you can put a pillow under your forehead, which will serve as a support. Or to get tired less try to rest your forearms, and not just your hands. In fact, placing only your hands, you risk not lasting more than two minutes, especially if you are not trained. We also advise you to lift your face often, otherwise, the blood will go to your head and you would risk feeling faint.

But if yoga is your favorite sport, this position will be a breeze for you!

Why should you try the wheelbarrow position (at least once in your life)?

Because, like many of the Kamasutra positions, the wheelbarrow allows you to have sex by stimulating new parts of the body and therefore to experience new sensations, to awaken the senses by putting them into play differently. If, having sex for months (or years) in the Missionary position, your senses are a little bit asleep, try to give them a hit of life by performing the wheelbarrow position, you will see that it works!

The variants to be tempted

The position of the wheelbarrow can have different variations, depending on the position of support or the height where you put your hands or elbows. For example, if the woman has her arms fully stretched. The man lifts her pelvis and the woman fastens her legs behind the partner's back, who supports her with his arms.

To make the wheelbarrow position less acrobatic, you can also rest your elbows on the bed, instead of on the ground. In this way, your body will be almost at the height of your partner's pelvis and you will not have to lift your back vertically.

In short, if you think that the acrobatic positions of the Kamasutra are not for you that you are not a great sportswoman, know that you can always adapt them to your physical condition.

### *The wheelbarrow (alternative)*
The woman is resting on her arms and on one knee. The man is on his knees, holding his partner by the pelvis and her unbent leg leans on his side. It is he who rhythms the movement. This position cannot be maintained throughout the whole intercourse

## The 10 Tantric Sex Positions
Taking new positions can help renew the passion. Before reviewing the best positions of tantric sex, it is necessary to follow some very specific preliminaries in order to achieve full physical and mental satisfaction. In this regard, partners during tantric love must find themselves in a condition of complete relaxation. They must observe and contemplate themselves. Only when this balance will be achieved, only when the outpouring of glances and breaths will be maximum, then and only then you can proceed. Tantra positions can help you get started the right way. These 4 main positions look like yoga positions for couples and will make you feel fused together:

• Lotus position: the most famous one, made a cult by Sting himself (who told the press that he could have tantric sex for more than 7 hours in a row. Not bad!). Him sitting, her sitting on his thighs wrapping him with her own legs and holding him in a hug while moving rhythmically. Looking into his eyes it's the key.

• Variant of the lotus position: sitting facing each other, legs intertwined to merge into the penetration.

• Position of the hot chair: him sitting on the chair and leaning against the backrest, her sitting on him with her legs leaning against his shoulders.

• Variant of the position of the hot chair: both kneeling, he behind her pushing from behind while she makes circular movements with her pelvis. Super hot.

### Lotus Position
Perhaps the best known among the tantric sexual positions to be exploited in bed is that lotus flower where the man stands cross-legged with the woman on top of him, crossing his thighs behind his partner's back to wrap him and look him intensely in the eyes.

### Lotus Variant
This basic tantric position can have several variations, such as the one where man and woman are sitting opposite each other and the legs intertwine almost as if to create a unique being perfectly fused together.

### Ground Position
The typical position with him sitting and her on top of him is great to try even lying on the floor, or with pillows to make the intercourse more comfortable.

## Tantric Positions With Chair
The most acrobatic lovers, who want to try new tantric positions, can also achieve pleasure with the help of a chair, where the seated man can welcome the woman who puts her legs over her partner's shoulders.

## Crouching
Among the best tantric sexual positions to try with a chair is also the one in which the woman is squatting over the man resting her feet on the edge.

## The Bomb
The tantric position of the bomb involves the man sitting on a chair and the woman on top of him, without touching the ground with her feet.

## Tantric Positions In Water
Tantra can also be safely put into practice in water, for example on a swimming pool, with the man sitting on the ladder and the woman crouched over him.

## Tantric Position In Bathtub
If you have a bathtub, you can try the classic tantric sexual position with hot water as an additional sexy and relaxing ingredient.

Tantric sex is the key to open the doors of pleasure, release sexual energy, allowing you to experience special sensations while experiencing very long intercourse times. This discipline of oriental origins changes the approach to sex, which is declined as a tool to achieve harmony of the senses, harmony of the couple, inner and outer balance, all passing from a unique and extremely captivating sensory experience.

# ANAL SEX

## The Anal Sex Positions to Try
The following description of each position is not intended to be the definitive "correct way to go." when trying something completely new, it is best to experiment in familiar and straightforward positions not to complicate the process. The correct part is crucial for anal beginners; It will help you get used to this exciting new form of stimulation and pleasure. Each of the following positions has its advantages and disadvantages, and each is suitable for newbies and newbies. Remember that most places are ideal for couples: any gender or sexual orientation. Remember, there is no wrong sexual position if it works for you and your partner. Feel free to adjust the settings described in this part to suit your specific needs, including your height, flexibility, comfort, and personal preferences.

### *Sitting Dog*
Lean forward from the lap dance position until your upper body is at right angles to his. Try facing a wall or another (sturdy!) Bench in front of you so that you have something to lean on or hold on to. That provides you with a

more extraordinary view of your buttocks and a better angle of penetration, especially if your penis curves away from your body. That is good for a less extreme version of the doggie style.

### Flying Doggie
In Flying Doggie, she kneels on all fours on the bed, and he stands (instead of kneeling) behind her. She brings her legs together, and his legs are on either side as he penetrates her from a little higher.

### Doggy Angle
When you lift your bum in the air and lower your head or head and shoulders, your body tilts perfectly to stimulate your G-spot, which can be more comfortable for some women than standing on all fours.

### Froggie
Froggie Position is a variation on cowgirl in which she crouches on her feet. That gives her more freedom to ride it vigorously and puts less strain on her knees, but she works for multiple muscle groups, so she has to be fit to keep it up. She can put her hands on her stomach in preparation. That position can be easier to achieve on the floor than in bed, depending on the firmness of the mattress and possible leverage.

### Reverse Froggie
Start in Reverse Cowgirl, stand up to crouch, sit straight, or lean forward, do most pushing work to get into this position. The woman must be fit, flexible, and have strong quadriceps to hold this position. Leaning forward, you can caress your partner's eggs and soft perineum; If he likes anal play, she can reach into his anus for stimulation and penetration. It can also be tilted backward for better skin contact and a different angle of penetration.

### Standing
When standing, both partners stand in the same direction, and he steps into her from behind. It can stand upright, leaning against a wall, or leaning against a piece of furniture.

### Upright Missionary
She lies on her back in the upright missionary position; he sits on her knees and stands between her legs. She bends her knees and rests her feet on his chest; in this position, he can stroke and squeeze her breasts or even pinch her nipples when he likes it; You can also easily reach and stimulate her clitoris with your hand or a vibrator. You will have a great view of the action in this position as you can see your penis going in and out. She can watch him penetrate her. and caress her breast and nipples. This can be an alternative to Missionary when taking the weight off her or in a less pretzel-like body position; it's also suitable for members of very different sizes or weights.

### Missionary L
He sits on his knees and moves between her legs; she lies on her back and puts her legs up in front of him so that they are perpendicular to the rest of her body and form an L at right angles to the torso and the rectum slightly straightens up and makes penetration a little easier. In Missionary, where your legs are bent back, you need to be pretty flexible to hold this position, so this may not

be a position for many women. It can last a long time. This position allows him a shallower penetration than other variations, which is good if he has a longer penis or if he doesn't like it too deep.

## Spoon and Fork

To test this variation, pairs should start in the spoon position. Next, she puts her left leg under his right leg and her right leg over it to wrap it around his waist. He can lower his arm to give himself. more leverage and more thrust. Like the spoon, this position creates shallower penetration and is ideal for men with long penises; However, many men find that they can push faster and with more enthusiasm. Since her body leans more towards him, kissing is more accessible in this position too.

## The Jockey Sex

Those women enjoy having their men in their corner and making the most of this type of sex. The woman must lie down in this position with her legs tight. The man would then come up behind you and sit with his knees bent.

He needs to lean over the back to get the best angle for pushing his penis inside your butthole and driving you insane with his rocking to and from movement. So, these are some of the best anal sex positions which you can surely try. Remember, it is essential to observe the proper rules, which we had discussed earlier. Practicing safe sex is crucial to ensure that both partners can benefit from it.

This is not the ultimate bible, as there are endless other positions that you can try. So come up with anything out of your mind. The only rule is that never stop having fun!

If you are up for a round of anal sex, you could try some of these positions and note down your experience. You will prepare better for the best sex experience of all time.

## Highchair

This is one of the powerful anal sex positions which is likely to give you both a lot of thrill. The woman needs to sit on a chair so that the butt must stick out of it. The guy then needs to stand behind. He could kneel down or even squat based on the elevation of the chair.

The man would grab his partner's waist and slowly push his penis in the anus. The in and out moment is sure to feel like a rocking chair and will drive both of you crazy with passion.

## Reverse Isis

In the reverse Isis position, he lies with his legs apart and slightly bent; she sits between his legs, with her face at his feet, leaning forward on his knees with her legs together. Until her breasts touch his legs, he can sit up to move into the doggy position.

## The Split

In The Split, she puts herself in the lap dance position, but instead of putting her legs between his, she puts them on either side of his, with your toes, which limits your ability to ride it hard. Keeping your legs together will further restrict your movements.

### The Burning Man
Yet another position wherein the man achieves the dominant role, and you could play the submissive lead.

The position is simple, but you would need a tabletop or even a sofa. The woman needs to lean on the top of the couch, table, or bed so that her anal end out. The man then spoons you from behind, and after enjoying some oral sex, he pushes his cock inside your hole. Therefore, it is essential to ensure that your table or sofa is such that it doesn't hurt you when leaning on it. Keeping a pillow or a blanket might be a good alternative.

This form of anal sex has the potential to get rough as your man could do all he wishes since you are bent on the table and can only moan and shriek in pleasure and pain. So, for those who love rough sex, this is

### YabYum
YabYum is a classic tantric sex position in which one partner sits on the other's lap and faces each other; However, it is generally taught and practiced as a position for vaginal penetration; it also works very well for anal penetration. The man is sitting with his legs slightly crossed, and the woman is sitting on his lap, encircling her legs around his waist and torso. You can use firm pillows under your thighs if you need more support for your legs. With his legs crossed, he can stand her in front of him. If you need back help, you can lean against the wall or the headboard. When she is lying on your lap, she can rise slightly above her knees, and you should bend her forward, pelvis forward to make your anus more accessible. He can hold the base of his penis to help her, and she can slowly lower herself onto him. That is a relaxing and meditative position. So once you are in it, you shouldn't feel any tension or tension. As you do this, adjust yourself to sink into place comfortably.

### The Chairman
Try entering YabYum on a chair, ottoman, sofa, or pillow on the floor. A comfortable chair or sofa can give men the back support they need. With a firmer surface under him and legs down, a man can feel firmer in this position, with more freedom of movement and a little more ability to squeeze gently. A man can hold his partner's hips and move his body up and down on his penis. If the partner is seated in a sufficiently broad chair, she can move her legs so that she straddles him but is not wrapped around his waist.

### Lap Dance
The edge of the bed, but it is best if both partners' feet can lightly touch the floor. The man is sitting on a chair, sofa, or ottoman, and his partner is astride him (with her back to him). He holds her legs apart, and she sits between his legs with her legs together. The closer she is to the ground, the easier she can achieve complete freedom of movement. That is a good position for couples where the woman is much smaller than the man.

### Tailgate
In surfing language, tailgate means paddling out into the ocean with your surfboard to catch a wave or follow someone else. She lies on her stomach in the tailgate position with her legs slightly apart. She, with his legs on either side of hers, penetrates her from behind. If he's having trouble getting in, she

84

can tilt her hips toward him for the first penetration and then lie down. Once inside of her, he pushes his legs together. He sets the tone in this position and takes care of the depth and rhythm of the penetration. You can also start in the Doggie Style, Doggie Angle, or Spooning position and quickly switch to them.

## Horizontal Tailgate

It starts in the seated tailgate position, and once stepped onto it, lean forward to lie on it with your legs outstretched (A). That allows for more skin-to-skin contact, and many women like to feel their partner's weight on them. It can also increase your partner's feeling of being "taken over." He can kiss her neck and ears and whisper sweet or naughty things to her (B). There are some downsides: a horizontal tailgate may not be feasible if he is taller and can't support his weight. Some women may also feel too cramped or uncomfortably immobilized regardless of their size. It has even less pressure.

## The Turtle Position

This position is for those couples who like to play the submissive-dominant game. The woman needs to be on her knees and then pull them inside. This position gives her hips a high arch, and the man could kneel and draw her waist towards him before pushing his penis in the anus and giving her a fun-filled ride.

This position can be uncomfortable for the woman, and you should be ready to improvise the moment you want to.

## Stallion

In stallion, she stands with her legs apart, then bends forward at the waist and leans on the bed (or other furniture), and he stands behind her. Stallion has all of the benefits of the doggie style with more strength as he has total leverage with his hips and legs. For some couples, this may work better than Flying Doggie due to its size and height. If she is feeling too much tension on her knees in other doggie positions, this is a better option for her. he can position his hips a little higher than hers and indirectly stimulate her G-spot when he penetrates her.

## The Pearly Gates

If you are looking for an anal sex position that could feel a little exciting, this is it. In this position, the man needs to lie down on his bed. He can spread apart his legs a little, but the feet should be pretty planted. The woman would now get on top of the man and face the same side. Make sure to position yourself in such a way that the man's penis could find the woman's butthole, and he could slowly but steadily make an entry and please you thoroughly.

This position allows for a lot of cuddling, foreplay, and even fingering as well. So, feel free to elevate your senses before getting downright dirty and rough.

## Side Saddle

She lies on her side with straight knees, legs together, and at an angle to the body. On his knees, he steps into her from the side. Think of Side Saddle as a combination of doggie style and spooning. Because of its unique position, you have the most control over-penetration.

### The Y
Starting in the side saddle, she moves her upper leg up to rest on her shoulder, essentially creating a side split with her body. Unlike the side-saddle, the Y requires strength and flexibility from her side, and some women can be difficult; or This variant allows both partners better access to your vulva and a good view of the penetration.

### Stairway to Heaven
Stairway to Heaven is the standing position performed on the stairs. Ladders provide handrails (and possibly a nearby wall) for support and balance, adding stability and leverage to both partners—the right height.
undoubtedly an excellent position to try.

### Over the Edge
Imagine Over the Edge as a horizontal tailgate on the edge of the bed. She lies on her stomach, her head, shoulders, and upper body hang over the edge of the bed, her hands are on him, he is lying on top of her, her hands also flat on the floor. Both partners in this position may have a head frenzy (of blood and oxygen), which in some may exacerbate sexual sensations. Your breasts won't tighten in this position, and you may feel less claustrophobic. That works best when your bed is relatively low off the floor.


## Best Kamasutra Positions for Anal Sex

### The Pivot Position
The girl, during intercourse, turns like a horizontal wheel around a vertical axis right around the male. The male caresses her and pinches her breasts, benefiting from those positions. For her part, the reclining man, whose penis uses her as a pivot in blood and flesh, can fondle her chest. She just takes up the length of his penis by squirming and raising herself a bit; she needs to believe in herself. The position of the pivot" will allow women and men to enjoy a great mental focus. For males who have begun to practice sexual continence, that is the reason why this position is proposed.

### Seesawing Position
Sitting slightly in front of the thighs of the male, she only takes part of his penis so that the length inserted alternately can be easily managed by either of them. She can stroke the male's legs kneeling; he comes to reach her halfway or perhaps behaves as though he was going to withdraw entirely by supporting himself on his arms and making quick thrusts with his pelvis, living her almost fully to be able to enter her open vagina again, and that is very wet in this position. This gives her an incredibly good upward massage.

### The Buttering Position
The man, firmly planted in the rear opening, turns around as if he is in a position to support his body on the palms as well as on the tip of the toes. In this position, in addition to circular ones, the male can make come-and-go movements. The female will not remain passive but will respond with smooth pelvic movements based on those created by the male.

86

The male provides the female with an exceptional massage of her G spot in the "buttering" position so that not many females can resist such stimulation without getting a deep orgasm (we're talking about non-ejaculatory orgasm, of course) as such. If the male thinks that he is approaching the orgasm, he must stop moving and concentrate his attention on the central position 3to be able to sublimate the sexual energy. This is also available to the woman.

### The Hidden Door Position
The male lies on the female. She encompasses his thighs, ready to take him as much as the hilt. He insinuates himself deeply and softly anchored within her, where he cuddles her, stroking her back, hips, and breasts. She draws up her spreads and legs them somewhat to have the freedom to give her vulva to the g absolutely to the needs of her lover even more.

Nevertheless, in an analogous situation, if he knows she loves anal penetrations, the male lover can even entertain himself with his lover's anal opening in case he knows she loves anal penetrations. Here the female can relax in the very best way as well as the male has full control over the penetration of his penis into the hot and constricted opening, which she gives him with confidence and affection.

This position is the right to lift the sexual energy and sublimate it in pure love. To achieve this elevated emotion—love that is pure, the lovers have not to focus on genital gratification during this position, but they have to concentrate their attention on the heart area and be aware of the flying feeling that this position actually creates if the lovers later let themselves to concentrate on the heart area.

### The Caress of the Bud Position
Lying on the stomach and the legs interlaced, the male and the female turn to each other with their backs. However, for a few males whose thick and short penis can only be flexed with difficulty, the particular effect of this position can be quite painful. The female, who retains her balance with a single-arm now facing her lover and who is assisted in the continuation of the position, the female, who maintains her balance with a single-arm now facing her lover and who's supported on the male's body, is titillated at the entrance to her vagina by the glans. Obviously, this is only foreplay to deeper coitus. The male can inserts his erect penis into the vagina by turning gently to one side. The vagina is now ready to get it in its totality.

For those lovers who are beginners in the art of sexual energy management, this position is the right one. The position of "the caress of the bud" allows lovers the ability to be much more mindful of the strength of pleasure and to reduce it by stopping the movement when they think they are near the climax. The sexual energy they have to concentrate their attention on is in the middle of the forehead for sublimation. This will trigger a clear-minded state in both lovers, which will allow them to regulate sexual power as well as to sublimate far higher energies.

### The Seesaw Position
Lovers are facing one another. The male then brings the female to the level of his waist. She's always able to catch him by his arms or around his neck,

87

maybe. Penetrated by the entire length of the penis, she allows the erect shaft to slip through her narrow vagina. By squeezing her legs tightly around his waist, the male can press and embrace her very close to himself that she can simplify for him.

In this particular position, with the aid of the strength of her muscles, the penis massages the entire vagina, the female can make good going and coming movements in tune with those of her lover. Both women and men would experience immense joy in this way. To be able to stay away from the male's ejaculatory orgasm as well as the female's discharge orgasm, both lovers have to really direct the sexual energy along the spine towards the crown. In pure love and happiness, this will create a sublimation of simple energy.

### The Closed and Opened Ring Position

Here we have two complete submission positions, where the female gets the male and then the degree of its resemblance. According to his rhythm, he penetrates her effortlessly, entertaining himself by inserting and removing his penis, sometimes carefully and sometimes violently. An experienced woman in the art of lovemaking is going to use this position to swing gently and carefully with her own thighs on the thighs of her lover and to send her vagina, which is really being bombarded from below.

The closed and opened ring sex position helps the male to be even more conscious of the strength of pleasure and to reduce it by stopping the movements when he knows he's approaching the climax. Both lovers have to concentrate their attention in the center of the forehead for sublimation, their sexual energy. This will trigger a clear-minded state in both lovers, which will allow them to concentrate their focus to sublimate.

### The Ripe Mango Plum Position

The male plunges into her with great sensitivity to begin spinning motions with his penis even more aggressively, and that is pretty fascinating for both lovers. He sits over his lover to penetrate deeper, spreads his legs, and inserts his penis into the swollen mango plum, which is well supplied by the adroit massage with blood. For both lovers, this sexual pose is an extremely arousing one. The elevated pelvis position of the female allows the sexual energy to "rush" into the region of the thyroid gland. This can cause an exceptionally high form of orgasm in females.

To stay away from his ejaculatory orgasm or maybe her discharge of orgasm, the male needs to stop his movements as he thinks he or maybe she's getting close to the climax. This sex position helps the ripe mango plum to sublimate sexual energy into ingenuity and purity.

### The Door Ajar Position

The male will keep his lover by the hips, after which he gently pushes it back between the legs of his lover. The female, pivoting slightly to the side, reaches around the neck of her lover in order not to lose any of the lengths of the penis. Well lubricated from other positions, the vulva is now moistened, allowing the penis to slip easily, massaging the vagina's sides. To be able to keep away from the ejaculatory orgasm of the male as well as the extreme orgasm of the female, both lovers have to concentrate their attention in the forehead. They will become much more aware of the sexual energy in this particular way.

### The Face to Face Position

Leaning on her soles and palms, the woman raises her pelvis so that the male can insert his penis into her vagina. He can capture his lover's waist with a single or even despite both hands while he has kneeled. This position helps lovers to search for each other to explore how their lust mounts and express their affection. The woman can gently push her pelvis, tuning her movement with the going and coming motions of the male. She can stretch her legs primarily to be able to take up the entire length of the penis of her partner.

If the male thinks he's getting close to the ejaculatory climax, he's going to stop moving and concentrate his focus in the central position to be able to sublimate the sexual energy. This is also available to the woman.

### The Top Position

This will make her lie on her back, sustained and blocked by the thighs of the male who penetrates her in a controlled press up, tightly massaged on the sides of the female, taking up the entire length of the penis. At the moment, he allows his weight to fall on her a lot more as he wants to feel a lot more satisfaction. The woman can feel him more deeply at exactly the same time. This position gives both lovers intense gratification and amplifies the sexual force. This is why it does not start contact with beginners in the art of lovemaking with sexual continence. Both lovers must concentrate their attention on the central position.

When the woman thinks that her lover gets close to the climax, she must avoid the movements of the male and simply press firmly on the middle of the forehead with her thumb. Therefore, his attention will be taken to the forehead region from the genital area, which helps to increase the sexual tension along the backbone.

## Conclusion

If you're up for a round of anal sex, you may try any of these options and, as always, keep track of your experience. It will better prepare you for the best sex experience of your life.

# DIRTY TALK

## Benefits of Dirty Talking

Talking dirty during the sexual activity help to lose inhibitions and to be more "unconscious" during the sexual act. When we reach orgasm, the brain releases oxytocin, a hormone that reduces stress and lowers the risk of depression. And when we are more relaxed, we are also more likely to say what we like under the sheets. We don't worry if what we say is out of place or if our moans sound like the sounds of a dying dog. Free from anxiety, we only think about reaching the pinnacle of pleasure and, for this, we are more open-minded.

They increase the excitement and intensify the experience of the relationship.

They allow you to take control ... or lose it, depending on your taste: using dirty language during sex helps to establish the roles that the two lovers assume and to understand better what you want. Telling, driving, dominating...They help women to overcome the "good girl" complex, that sort of prejudice for which a woman must be good and quiet, otherwise she will never be a good wife and her reputation will be ruined.

Women let you go: Saying bad words in bed will make you feel free to express your sexuality, satisfy your desires and feel good about yourself, without trapping yourself in the categories of 'slut' or 'bride'. Speech is a tool that denotes a certain independence. Free yourself from all these labels.

Last but not least, they allow us to free ourselves from taboos and feed our sexual fantasies, creating new ones. Talking dirty therefore becomes an opportunity to reveal our dark sides and experience things we would not normally do. "Insulting" your partner is not really thinking what you say, but simply putting one of these fantasies into action through language.

In summary, this practice can be very useful to dissolve or "break free". Some of us suffer from educational or religious beliefs, and sometimes in bed they may have trouble expressing themselves as they would like. Of course, this can happen like a game, in cases of deeper closure: erotic themed jokes are fine, as well as laughter with certain vulgar words that we will never pronounce in other contexts.

Moreover, dirty talk can be useful to explore one's sexuality and express, even as a joke, your fantasies to the partner. Which in fact can also lead to their realization, if you wish. Do not overlook the fact that the intimacy of the couple could also benefit. But even for this practice, rules are needed.

# 3 Golden "Rules" To Not Exaggerate

## *1. Always be in agreement*

Consensuality is fundamental in any area of sex. Discuss with your partner first to see if dirty talk is something you can practice or one side doesn't like. For some people, silence is golden.

## *2. Set Your Stakes*

Although it is not a practice that is part of the BDSM, you can think of agreeing on a safety word for dirty talk too, to avoid going too far. In general, however, it is good to agree with your partner on what you can and cannot talk about, what kind of language to use or what fantasies to use.

It means that for you, as a couple, this practice is not taboo in itself, but you need rules. Much better than jumping without a parachute into an experience that can be extremely unpleasant for some.

## *3. No insults*

It can happen that, in a moment of passion, you let yourself go and say something inappropriate. It can be understood, it can be justified. But transcending the rules of behavior could be one of those stakes we mentioned.

Insults - especially of a sexist nature - can be intolerable even in **these contexts.**

# Dirty Talk to Woman

Have you at any point had dirty considerations about a young lady? Have you at any point needed to advise her precisely what you need to do to her until she's hot and sweat-soaked and prepared to hook your garments off?

All things considered, if I know most men, you've likely kept those considerations and words to yourself. You may have even retained them while you were connecting with a young lady for dread that she may get outraged and leave. However, try to keep your hat on; she's hanging tight for you to break out the dirty talk. So I'll talk about properly dirty talk with ladies and take your and her experience to the next level.

I stared at her for a minute. Her eyes darted and began to dance around the room, but I directed her gaze downward as an escape from my fascination.

We discussed some mundane topics, but the words were evaporating into cloudiness of vitality and trade of vibes. Yet, the subtext trade couldn't have been clearer. Her students started to extend, and her palms were getting sweat-soaked.

I snatched the rear of her head and pulled her toward me until my lips were inches from her ear. I realized she could feel my hot breath stinging the side of her face. I started kneading her scalp. I began to talk from my stomach, guaranteeing my voice was, in any event, an octave lower than typical. I seized a tight her other arm. I revealed to her that if we weren't in an open scene, I would punch her in a bad position, pull her hair back and kiss her everything over her neck while I ripped her garments off. Also, before the night finished, she realized that I was a long way from all talk. And keeping in mind that I was strolling the walk, I kept on dirtying conversation with her until she wanted to discharge the creature inside.

I've had a ton of involvement in dirty talk when connecting with young ladies or sexting them. Maybe to an extreme, some could state. Yet, I can let you know no ifs, ands, or buts is that ladies love sex, ladies love dirty talk.

However, such a significant number of men are just hesitant to push the sexual envelope. They are worried about the possibility that the lady will get awkward, or she will dismiss them, or they will become uncomfortable because they are wandering into a new area. In any case, in light of your faltering, I will share one of my preferred Mark Twain cites:

"Quite a while from now you will be increasingly disillusioned by the things that you didn't do than by the ones you did. So lose the anchor. Sail away from the sheltered harbor. Catch the exchange winds your sails. Investigate. Dream. Find."

If you've perused my pieces previously, you've heard me talk about my dread of "imagine a scenario where?" Cultivating this dread is how I had the option to wreck approach tension. Getting dismissed, extinguished, missing the mark... everything can be highly excruciating (until you, in the end, understand that you're realizing, that is), however nothing. I amount to nothing, and it is more agonizing than lament. Realizing that as a man, you could've accomplished something; you could've acted, yet you didn't do anything.

So sail away from your protected harbor and take a risk for once in your life. You have no clue how a lot of a young lady will regard you. What's more, you might be astounded at the outcome. Also, in particular: do it for yourself.

Fortunately for you, dirty talk is anything but difficult to learn and a great spot to begin if you need to start stretching the limits more.

Stage 1: *BE A SEXY MAN*

If you're attempting to dirty talk to a lady, you've never laid down with, or hell, a lady you haven't had more than one discussion with, the possibility can be overwhelming. It very well may be not very comforting just to consider it. The truth of the matter is, when most men attempt to dirty talk to ladies, they appear to be:

*Unpleasant*

*Clumsy*

*Uncaring*

*Excessively Aggressive*

In any case, they fall off in these ways for reasons that you may not think. It's positively not because ladies don't care for dirty talk. Instead, they should prepare for dirty talk.

If you put on a show of being excessively forceful: This implies you didn't appropriately set up a young lady to get sexual. It is primarily a problem for men who are dark-skinned.

If he is perceived as too forceful or engaging in dirty talk, he will be directly in line with that recognition, sending her into auto-rejection. To truly connect with a young lady, you must first get her in the right frame of mind.

If you put on a show of being obtuse: This implies you shifted the state of mind to sexual when there was excessive "well disposed" of a vibe, or if you were profound plunging her and she was trusting in you. If a young lady is disclosing to you a genuine anecdote about how she lost her dearest youth little dog and you begin talking about how you need to get her bare, she'll feel like you're attempting to utilize her.

If you put on a show of being clumsy: This implies you set an awful point of reference with the young lady, and your being sexual just left the blue. Or on the other hand, it means that you haven't gathered up enough social speed, and you're conveying uncomfortable vibes.

If you put on a show of being dreadful: This implies your non-verbal communication is clumsy, you haven't developed enough social confirmation in her eyes, you didn't give her plausible deniability, and additionally, your style/game is excessively powerless.

Usually, I wouldn't say I like to praise silver projectiles, but on this occasion, I can say that you can fix these visual cues by doing something: improving and adjusting your provocative vibe.

Suppose you're perceived as being overly forceful. In that case, your provocative vibe is powerful, and you need to dial it back with more energy and make her giggle/feel quiet to open herself up to your advances further.

If you're experiencing being unbalanced or frightening, your attractive vibe is excessively frail. You have to take a shot at hitting young ladies with your provocativeness directly off the bat. You are putting on a show of being overly "safe," and a young lady doesn't consider you to be a darling natural alternative.

If you're experiencing being inhumane, your provocative vibe is confounded. You have to associate with the young lady on an enthusiastic level and cause her to feel like she's interfacing with you. And afterward, you can alleviate the strain with a joke or some light prodding and begin to get sexual.

Stage 2: *SUBTLE DIRTY TALK EARLY IN AN INTERACTION*

Except if a young lady is already warmed up and ready, you'll need to start the dirty talk in a light and subtle tone. I was as of late bantering to and from with a young lady. We talked about work and snickering about entertaining proficient stories – nothing too naughty... until I tossed some unobtrusive sexuality in with the general mishmash. I quit snickering, took a gander at her as though I needed to get her, and to maul kiss her at that moment. Then I got a slight grin all over.

Me: But that is only my regular everyday employment. You couldn't deal with what I do around evening time...

Her: [a sultry look in her eye] Oh definitely... and what might that be?

Me: I'm a janitor. Because I get dirty, I make things wet, and I deeply inspire individuals.

Furthermore, this line (and lines like these) did an astonishing thing for me. It was an explicitly charged line, so it made her go and in an increasingly sexual outlook. Be that as it may, after I said it, she wanted to chuckle because it's only a clever line too. So it deals with two levels. First, great inconspicuous sexuality imparts sexual subtext while keeping the outside layer of correspondence light and fun. Since she's giggling, she can't blame you for being unpleasant or excessively sexual; however, since you did offer a sexual remark, she sees you more in the sweetheart casing. Sexual jokes, when utilized well, can be advantageous assets for pushing cooperation ahead.

Stage 3: *ESCALATE TOUCH*

If you've been taking part in light sexual chitchat, this is an ideal opportunity to begin contacting her. You ought to be energetically getting her while you exchange, and as you start to profound jump her and make the connection more substantive, you should begin utilizing the more delayed types of touch.

Stage 4: *TURN UP THE HEAT*

If you've built up an association with her, turn up the sexual warmth when she least anticipates it. Don't do it if she's revealed to you a genuinely charged story and is searching for your approval, yet do it when you are talking about yearnings like travel, or are kidding around to alleviate the strain, or are simply examining a progressively unremarkable theme. For instance:

Her: And that was the insane story of my excursion to Bali!

You: Wow, that was a powerful story! I'm going to call up National Geographic at present! Also, after all that, here we are in an arbitrary American jump bar. Isn't this the fantasy?

Her: Haha, I know, right... this is life!...

94

You: [grabbing her arm, and inclining indirectly by her ear] Sarah, I need you to know, if we weren't right now, be kissing all over your neck at present, sliding my hands down your body and grasping a firm your hips. Also, I'd be beginning...

And afterward, you pull back, staring at her for a second, and later, keep talking regularly. And after that, propose setting off to a calmer spot or getting a nightcap or setting off to an after gathering, or whatever else goes to your head.

Short note: if it's truly on, you don't need to return to the ordinary discussion. You can disclose to her that you folks can get it going and leave at that moment. So this should be founded on your judgment.

Stage 5: *THE AMAZING "NO SEX" LINE*

I took in this line from a characteristic companion of mine. When I initially began utilizing it, its viability bewildered me. Furthermore, all the more stunning was that the more smoking the young lady was, the better the line became.

So it goes this way: while you're on the stroll back to your place or her place – or if it's a lesson when you show up at your goal – you stop the young lady and get a natural look all over. Then you look her dead in her eyes and summon up each ounce of sexuality that you have in your body.

We should make one thing straight...

Young ladies are sexual animals. Young ladies love sex. Young ladies consider sex, possibly more than you do. Young ladies, ladies, anything you desire to allude to the more pleasant sex as – they are not these unadulterated, chastised animals numerous in the media describe them.

I trust you knew this, yet I needed to ensure we agreed. What's more, since you know this, you ought to likewise realize that each young lady appreciates a touch of sexting now and then, mainly while she's ovulating. It's science.

Why You're Getting No Sexts

If you're perusing this article and thinking, "Gee, I wonder why I never get any sexts from young ladies?" then you've gone to the perfect spot. You're not getting any sexts because you're presumably doing one of a couple of things wrong.

Issue 1: *Attraction Type*

You may not be making enough fascination. Not the "Goodness, he's charming and perhaps I'll let him take me on a couple of dates" sort of fascination. I'm talking the "oh crap! For what reason am I following this outsider into his condo" some kind of sexual fascination.

If she's not explicitly into you, you most likely won't get any sexts, exposed pictures, or dirty talking from her. Instead, you need to stir her to get filthy writings and photographs from a young lady. You can't simply pull in her. She needs to effectively consider your rooster somewhere inside her before she'll effectively draw in you in sexting. Furthermore, unmistakably, this is simpler after you've laid down with a young lady...

Issue 2: *No Sex for You*

You may not be getting sufficiently laid. It's constantly more uncomplicated to get stripped pictures and dirty writings from young ladies you've laid down with previously. You'll generally be playing a daunting task if you're attempting to get things warmed up before laying down with her. It's conceivable, however, more complex.

Issue 3: *Tactless Thirsty Dudes*

You should know how to talk dirty with her appropriately. Instead, you go from "0 to 100" way too rapidly. Rather than preheating the broiler, you're excessively ravenous (or parched). You toss it in on sear and afterward overlook the stove miss when attempting to take it out. You have no tolerance or class.

Ladies love men of activity. They love men who follow what they need, done in the best possible way. Continuously be a man of honor. You shouldn't ever appear to be an audacious or inconsiderate social retard with no channel.

For instance, this is terrible content to send to a young lady:

"Decent gathering you the previous evening, can hardly wait to f**k you sideways in the not-so-distant future."

There is no trade. There is no such thing as a tease. There isn't any sizzle. You appear to be thirsty.

This young lady will lose the fascination she had for you, if any whatsoever. She will think you think she is a prostitute and disregard you.

### The most effective method to Talk Dirty to Girls Over Text (and ideally get some provocative shots)

*Cautioning*: The accompanying sexting models are very immediate, and we would prefer not to appear hostile. We accept that a man ought to endeavor to be however much gentlemanlike as could be expected and approach each lady with deference and profound respect. In any case when it goes to the room, indeed, isn't tied in with getting dirty?

*Here you go*:

### Be Playful and Tactful, But Slow Down Until You Know Her

Presently we talked about being parched and utilizing class to get her heated up. Everything is situational, and once you know a young lady, you can pull off significantly more than with a young lady you don't know excessively well.

There is a scarcely discernible difference with a gradually done idea. You, despite everything, need to be the energizing sort of man she'll be content with. In this way, you need to be prudent, however energetic simultaneously truly.

For instance, with a young lady you had pretty recently met the previous evening or a day or two ago, you could begin a discussion off explicitly with something like this:

"Great to meet you the previous evening... that provocative minimal bum of your is going through my head... completing no work today; you're a horrible impact on me!"

This model is fun-loving, and she'll appreciate the tease. You'll likewise certainly disclose to her you're a sexual man, not some pleasant, exhausting fellow – the sort of fellow she's presumably exhausted with.

You can genuinely begin things rapidly. This is a genuine case of a quick conversation with a young lady you've already gotten physically involved with:

You: "Well, it's Thursday evening, I'm off work, and I'm so horny when I consider you... what can I do?"ha

Her: "Get some ice?"

You: "Senseless young lady, that is mischievous. You weren't honored with hips like that to no end... get the decent clothing, some red lipstick, and get here at this point!"

This young lady will come over and go through an exquisite night ass exposed with you, as long as she doesn't have any too squeezing plans. You were reckless, however diverting. You caused her to feel hot and overwhelmed. You didn't put on a show of being a wet blanket. It means by which you dirty content.

### Start From the Beginning

Presently, the ideal approach to begin a dirty messaging discussion is to start from the earliest starting point. Be that as it may, you can't be an awkward wet blanket in doing as such. You can begin a discussion with a, to some degree, sexual vibe. It is because many folks abstain from being lively and sexual for the most part.

Start with the light wicked stuff and prop up from the absolute first content. Then consistently attempt to transform things into a sexual insinuation, regardless of whether it's cheesy. You don't need to talk about twisting her over a work area in the senior member's office to stimulate her.

For instance:

Her: "Hello you, how's your day going?"

You: "Gracious hello gingersnap... a touch of exhausting to be straightforward. Need some fervor today... "

Her: "Really? What sort of energy :)"

You: "Idk, perhaps an agreeable house cleaner who's does all that I ask... "

Keep the vibe fun and coy from here. You can keep sexting, or you can push for a meetup.

You May Offend Her

You will, in the long run, annoy her. Or, on the other hand, one of your "hers" will get irritated. You will be dirty messaging, and she will get resentful. This is fine. Don't be a colossal bitch and start saying 'sorry' in a needy way. Mellow outplay things cool. She may simply be trying you.

In any case, you have to give a slight expression of remorse. One approach to do as such:

Her: "that was extremely discourteous"

You: "Ahhhh I didn't offend you really awful, did I? Ugghhh fine, you get one punish and that is it... "

You acknowledge and recognize her annoyance, but you refuse to submit to her will. She, despite everything, regards you, and you've kept up her fascination.

## Jumping Deep – Dirty Texting for Experts

If you're a virgin and like to remain as such, you won't have any desire to keep understanding this. Notwithstanding, if you're prepared to take your sexting to the following level – read on.

*Here are a couple of increasingly master dirty messaging tips:*

*Running The Questions Game Over Text*

You should, as of now, be running "the inquiries game" on pretty much every first date. It's the most straightforward approach to plunge into more profound subjects and take a sexual discussion. Young ladies love that poop.

It's additionally a simple method to take a messaging discussion to a sexting discussion. Here's the specific system you should utilize:

You: "so wanna play a game."

Her: "Umm, sure."

You: "Cool inquiries game. Three inquiries each, yet you need to answer sincerely. No falsehoods or BS. You can't rehash the inquiry another person previously posed."

Her: "Haha, alright, however you ask first."

You: "I'm a man of honor. Women consistently start things out."

Presently a dominant part of the time, she'll battle you on this. That is fine. You can contend somewhat to and from. She may ask first, or she may "make" you.

If she asks first, answer every one of her inquiries genuinely and give her criticism if they are exhausting. If they are sexual, you're set. If she gives you exhausting ones (and is a held young lady) and you reply, you then mirror her inquiries while including a touch of edge. When she answers, give criticism and afterward cycle two. She may start to sexualize, or she may not. When you find a workable pace second round, you do.

If she "makes" you ask first, you can turn it on her rapidly:

You: "Well, I was going to get along, yet since you're in effect so obstinate..."

Try not to hang tight for her reaction:

You: "1. What number of men have placed their rocket into your pocket?"

You: "2. Do you like being commanded in bed?

You: "3. What's the one sexual thing you've for the longest time been itching to attempt yet never had the nerve to do?"

These are the cash questions. You need to find a workable pace in the game. They are what is important. So – regardless of if she goes first, you go; first, the vibe isn't sexual...

You need to find a workable pace. She might be shy; however, she'll reply. Flippantly get down on her about anything that doesn't sound genuine. Spitball a piece on her answers, then state

You: "Your turn."

She'll ask you, in any event, a couple of sexual inquiries, generally every one of the three. The answer truly, yet offer to warn her if anything is "as well" odd or insane before advising her (model: you've had 200 sexual accomplices).

Run one progressively adjust and pose two sexual inquiries dependent on her answers (model: What turns you on the most? How would you generally come?). Toss in an investigation dependent on her youth too. You need it to be sexual yet light. Something like:

You: Did you ever find a good pace greatest pound in middle school?

She'll reply. After two rounds, you ought to have enough things to be content about. First, let the inquiries game part of the sexting vanish.

In the wake of making her warm-up, you can request nudes if you think all is good and well.

### Messaging Her to Orgasm

You can utilize this after the inquiries game or in a different circumstance. For example, if you have a young lady who is sexual from the hop, a young lady you've laid down with previously, or a young lady with whom you've appropriately raised the convo, you can calmly offer to walk her through a climax.

When she's somewhat worked up, from some sexting, you can say:

You: If you ask pleasantly, I may let you have a climax.

Her: Umm, not certain what you're talking about, however sure

You: Say please and evacuate your jeans.

Her: Ok and please

You: Good young lady. Presently envision I'm there...

You: over you. I've nailed you down against the bed. I'm going to take you while you squirm and groan in delight. You feel a shiver between your legs as my hand contacts you. I get a clenched hand brimming with your hair and pull you close before kissing you profoundly. My fingers go through your hair as we kiss.

You: Then I get you and through your hands behind your back and curve you over. SMACK. You feel my hand gives your rear-end a firm smack. You whence as you groan. You feel a sting, however a lovely sentiment as well. So I take my belt and limit your options together.

Her: gracious wow

You: you need more?

Her: yesses

You: I push your face into the pad and pull my hand back to punish you once more... this time hard. You howl in torment; however, the cushion suppresses your groans. I instruct you to quiet down and take it like a decent young lady.

You: I flip you over and push you on your knees. I stand up and look at you without flinching before making you suck my hard chicken as I stand. You take my hard cockerel in my mouth as I powerfully get your hair. I begin to push a more significant amount of my chicken in your mouth as you choke.

Her: ahhh, this is acceptable.

You get the idea, folks.

You simply keep messaging her dirty until she says she intends to come. Then tell her you haven't let her in yet. After a few more sex texts, you conclude with:

You: "Cum. Presently."

The key is to warm her up before finding a good pace, reveal to her you'll make her come. When she's warm, be extremely unequivocal and prevailing in your writings. Then don't let her come until after the peak of your sexual story. That is when you utilize the last content.

Don't hesitate to request naked photographs, mainly if she came.

## Requesting Photos, The Right Way

A few young ladies will send you photographs unexpectedly. A few young ladies will never send pictures. A few young ladies will send photos to folks they've engaged in sexual relations with. A few young ladies will spam photographs to everyone.

If you've warmed her up through content, you are in a situation to request photographs. When she's warmed, you can pull off pretty much anything as long as you don't send "nudes" or something weak like that.

In any case, possibly you've engaged in sexual relations with a young lady yet haven't been sexting a lot. It would be best if you got nude photographs of her; however, you might not have the opportunity to put resources into a lot of sexting. In addition, she's not the sort to send nudes for reasons unknown or unexpectedly.

Whenever you shag her, offer it to her great multiple times and be harsh with her. Ensure you finish a piece sweat-soaked and exhausted. As you spend, you'll need to turn over and tap your chest. She'll move her head on your chest, and you'll cuddle a piece.

Please give her a light kiss on the temple and gradually recapture your breath. Then commendation whatever piece of her body you need photographs of, yet state it in an exasperated way:

You: "God, you have a decent screwing ass."

Or then again...

You: "Fuck, your tits are great."

You then slap her rear end and get her tit. Delicately, you would prefer not to intrude on the post-coital cuddles.

What's more, recall – the commendation must be veritable.

She won't overlook it, mainly if you screwed her right.

Presently, you may discover she sends you a photograph of her rear end as well as tits inside seven days of this event (once more, contingent upon how well you screwed her). If she doesn't, you have set yourself up to request a bare.

Start a discussion. It very well may be ordinary, yet ensure things are somewhat perky, then bring it up:

You: "For reasons unknown, that bum of yours won't leave my brain. It's screwing tormenting me. I can't rest. I can't eat ;)."

Her: "Haha, that is not my shortcoming. You're the wicked kid ;)."

You: Ahh, well, I can't deny that; however, I do know a pic or three of that bum may help with the entire eating and resting."

She may not send them immediately, yet she will in the end because you asked pleasantly.

One key thing to recollect: if you've found a workable pace in discussion with a young lady, you can and often should stack these dirty messaging tips. For instance, you can begin by running the inquiries game to sexualize the discussion. Then the idea to walk her through a climax. When she finishes, you could demand a couple of nude photographs as a much obliged.

Make sure that your agree on the risk level. Don't force her to do something that scares her too much.

The easiest way to pick the sex adventure is to have the woman share her fantasy and then you jointly pick one that meets her expectations.

Just talking about it will draw you closer together as a couple and help to turn her on. She may even have a no-touch orgasm by getting involved!


### 3rd Tip. How To Fully Enjoy It.

Once you have made your plan then follow through on it. Don't put it off. Take a dry run on it by talking her through the steps. Again, this may turn her on so much that you quit talking and have some fun! There's nothing wrong with that!

Cast your abandons to the wind. Check everything out and plan every detail. Then just go for it! Risk is part of the adventure as long as it is calculated risk!

## 4th Tip. Hot To Multiply Your Enjoyment Thereafter.

You could decide to video your encounter. Then you can enjoy it thereafter. Also, this now sets the standard for what you can do in the future. You can have many pleasant (and hot) moments rehearsing what happened.

She could also enjoy some residual orgasms where she plays today and enjoys great climaxes days later - even without touch! Take advantage of that free fun!

Start today and have your great adventure. Remember, the more combinations of fantasies, games, and techniques will determine your excitement level.

Good sex is great, but is "good enough" sex really good enough? Often people who have been sexually involved with each other for a long period of time may find that their sex lives fall into a little bit of a rut - it's fine, but it could be better sex. And the same can be true for some couples who are just starting out; there may be a little something missing, perhaps because they feel a little shy or unsure of themselves. Assuming penis health or another problem is not an issue, there's no reason that such couples shouldn't be enjoying even better sex - and one way to help achieve that goal could be to incorporate sex games into bedtime activities.

Sex games are a fun way to add a little spice back into sex play or to help "break the ice" among those still getting to know each other. There are dozens of games out there that a couple can use in search of better sex. Here are a few that they can consider to get themselves started:

- Strip anything. Almost everyone knows about strip poker, in which people play cards but instead of betting with money, they bet with pieces of clothing. But the fact is that there are numerous other games that can incorporate stripping. For example, get a pair of dice and have each person pick a number - say, five for him, eight for her. Roll the dice. Every time a five comes up, he takes off a piece of clothing and the same for her when eight is rolled. Or to make it more fun, let her take off his piece of clothing when five is rolled and he take off hers when eight is rolled.

- Distracted wooden tower. Take one of those stackable wooden towers and put it together. As with normal play, the trick is to remove pieces of the tower without it falling down. The challenge in this version is that as the player is trying to remove the piece, their partner is rubbing and massaging their genitals to distract them.

- Penis ring toss. The man picks out five sex positions and assigns each one a number, without letting the partner know what they are. He then stands with a firmly erect penis while the partner tosses five plastic hoops, trying to get them to land on his penis. If, say, three end up around the penis, they then have sex using whatever position was assigned the number three.

103

- Orgasm race. The partners masturbate each other, trying to make the other reach orgasm first. Vibrators and other sex toys may be used. Determine an appropriate prize for whoever wins - whether it's sexual, like getting to determine what sex position to use the next time they have sex or practical, like taking out the garbage.


- Sexy slips. Each partner takes several slips of paper and writes on each one of them something sexy he wants the other to do, e.g. "Tie me up with stockings" or "Service me orally at the breakfast table" or "Masturbate in front of me." Each partner draws a slip and has to follow the instructions. (If they are unwilling or unable to, they can pass - but they should talk about why they are reluctant to do it.)

Sex games are one route to better sex - but the best route involves being willing and able to communicate lovingly and openly (if tactfully) with a partner.

Made in the USA
Las Vegas, NV
20 March 2024

87480031R00059